Letter to Elizabeth

Toby Rompf

Letter to Elizabeth
Copyright © 2020 by Toby Rompf

All rights reserved. No part of this publication may be reproduced, distributed, or transmitted in any form or by any means, including photocopying, recording, or other electronic or mechanical methods, without the prior written permission of the author, except in the case of brief quotations embodied in critical reviews and certain other non-commercial uses permitted by copyright law.

Tellwell Talent
www.tellwell.ca

ISBN
978-0-2288-3851-7 (Hardcover)
978-0-2288-3850-0 (Paperback)
978-0-2288-3852-4 (eBook)

Chapter One

Henry awoke from another restless sleep, with the pounding of the seemingly unlimited shells and mortars still rattling around in his head. You would think that he would be used to it by now. It's been years since the war began, and if anything was inconsistent, it was the sounds of battle. The noise of tanks and bombs came and went throughout the years, sometimes from the east, sometimes from the west. Sometimes barely audible, and sometimes loud enough that everyone's eyes widened and they gripped whatever was around them. It would disappear for a period of time, and then just as you thought it would finally be over, they returned again with a vengeance.

It wasn't so much the noise; it was the lack of any rhythm in it. He remembered when he was younger, he and his wife had lived on the beautiful Rhine River. Three times a night, precise enough to set your watch by it, the tugboats would let fly a loud cry, letting the harbormaster know that they were coming in for a shift change. After a few months he almost looked forward to hearing it. A dull blast from the ships over an often-foggy river almost seemed romantic, even if the sound was loud and haunting. He had loved living there, and missed it dearly. Moving to the countryside to start his own practice seemed wonderful at the time, but all things considered, he wished he were back there now, back at that time. The only worry then was what they would spend the little money they had on, and often they just ended up cuddling together in front of a small fire in their apartment and munching on pretzels and pepperoni.

But the noise of war was altogether different. There was no rhythm in it. No romance. Nothing good came from that noise, only death and destruction. With each flash, with each bomb, came the realization that there would be more casualties, more children that would see neither their fathers nor mothers again. He hadn't slept properly for a while now.

He rose from his small bed to see his wife beside him, tossing ever so slightly. He loved her ever so deeply. Her beautiful brown hair, and the small dimples in each cheek when she smiled. She was almost everything to him. He couldn't remember what life was like before her, and shuddered with any thought as to what life would be without her.

They had met almost five years ago, in Düsseldorf. He was studying to become a doctor and she was taking a one-year course to become a nurse. They had only one class together during that time. It was unusual enough for women to go to school, but for them to actually attend a course with men happened rarely. It was only a general anatomy course, and the professor had asked for everyone to take a partner; it didn't take long as his eyes swept the room before they landed with a thud on Carmen. He almost tripped, trying to reach her in an attempt to ask her to become his partner. But with the woman and men separated in the large room, he only made it halfway before he could see that she had already found a partner in a short stocky girl beside her.

After that day, he had done everything he could to meet her. He was uncomfortable just coming out and stopping her somewhere to introduce himself. He really wanted the meeting to be organic, to be perceived as serendipitous, so he tried his best to make that happen. He followed her to each class, tried to bump into her in the hallways, dropped as many hints as he thought he could, but she still didn't do much in the way of acknowledging him. Finally with a deep breath, one winter's day, discarding his previous plans, he got up enough courage to walk up to her outside her dorm, and asked her if she would like to have lunch with him.

"I can't stop thinking about you," he told her, his words taking the form of steam as it hit the cold air. His face started to go red, as he wasn't as embarrassed but certainly feeling the pressure of a possible rejection. "I can't study or concentrate on anything but you; can you…I mean would you…like to have something to eat?"

He felt the hot blood rush into his cheeks and face and looked down toward her shoes, not able to hold her wonderful gaze.

"Well, Henry," she replied as she took her hand and lifted Henry's eyes to meet hers again. "That only took you six months."

She smiled at him and her warm glow seemed to leap into his whole body. He shuddered with excitement.

"I thought that you would have asked me that first day that we saw each other in our anatomy class. I've been waiting ever since."

Henry looked into her eyes and again started to feel flushed.

"I thought that you didn't want anything to do with me? I mean, I couldn't drop any more hints to you…. could I?"

Carmen smiled again, and chuckled in a sweet tone.

"A man isn't serious, unless he asks a lady face-to-face."

Wow. He had thought—and now knew—this would be the woman he would marry. He didn't tell her that out loud of course, but as he looked into her deep brown eyes, Henry knew that this would be the first, last and only woman he would ever love. They started dating immediately and the rest of the year flew by quickly. Henry's concentration on his studies waned somewhat, but he had a great partner in Carmen. She made sure that her new boyfriend maintained his grades and became an excellent study partner, even if she didn't understand all the details of his work. Once she was finished her year, she began to work at a local hospital as a nurse, and made sure Henry went to each and every course and did his best. Of course Henry was driven enough to get impressive grades, but he loved the fact that Carmen pushed him to strive higher.

It wasn't more than another year before both of them couldn't wait any longer, and they got married back on the family farm. With Carmen working almost full time, and Henry doing his best to pick up some extra cash when he could, they made ends meet, barely. They lived in bliss between the stress of studies and making sure enough food was on the table. But it was still bliss. And with the pending arrival of Henry's most beloved creation, life felt as if it couldn't get any better.

In his apartment, Henry rose to a sitting position on his bed and looked down to the corner of the room. There, lying on a small worn mattress was his two-year-old daughter. Looking at her sleeping peacefully under her favorite red blanket made his heart swell. Whatever hole his heart had, she filled, and filled until overflowing. He loved her so deeply. She was so beautiful, accepting everything they had endured so far with a smile and a trusting heart. She counted on her father for everything, and had no fear in her heart that he would ever let her down. They had named her Eden, because she was so perfect, and the beginning of their everything. The lack of food, of clothing, of heat, the war, and the work; all were put into perspective when looking into her eyes.

He remembered when Carmen was lying in the bed in the hospital room ready to give birth to their firstborn. Even though Henry was fully capable of delivering their future daughter, Carmen refused to let him. She smiled at him a few weeks before saying, "Henry, dear. Be a part of the miracle, be with me. Let some else take care of the delivery."

"But I'll make sure everything is done properly," Henry started. "Henry," Carmen stopped him before he could put his foot down. "Everything will be fine. Let the other doctors do their job, and you do yours." Carmen smiled and put Henry's hand on her stomach, letting him know with that small gesture that she wanted Henry to experience the birth of his child as a father, not as a doctor. Of course, Carmen was right. She was right more than she wasn't, Henry knew. He had experienced the wonderful miracle of his beautiful daughter being born, healthy and happy. That memory would never leave him, through the great times and the utter worst.

With a kiss on his wife's cheek, Henry dragged himself out of bed, dressing himself for another day. Munching on a day-old croissant, Henry crossed the abandoned streets to his small office. Unlocking the front door, he remembered as clearly as if it was yesterday, the day he had opened up his office for the first time. His wife was holding him, pregnant with Eden, and both were excited with the prospect of their first privately-owned doctor's office and outpatient clinic. They had dreams of administering health care to the small community they now lived in, building a little house on the river that wound its way to the north, and settling in for a long time. In the future they would dream of having two or three more children, all of them living forever in bliss and contentment.

Looking at the crooked yellow sign that now hung from his door, it told him as clearly as if someone kicked him in the stomach that things had progressed to a point where it didn't seem possible life would ever be normal again. "Guten Tag, Heinz", an old farmer commented as Henry was putting his keys in the lock. "Guten Tag," replied Henry, turning his head to the right to make sure he could hear him properly, and then allowing the key to release the lock and open the door. Both looked into each other's eyes for an instant, and both surmised that each was not really having a *good day*.

Henry entered his small doctor's office, looking around to make sure that everything was still in one piece. A fine layer of dust and soot seem to line his floor and desk each morning, creating a not-so-sterile area. The odd book or picture often found itself on the floor after a captain or general somewhere decided to target something far closer than necessary. Henry sat at his desk and looked into the picture of his wife that sat on his desk. It was an old black and white photograph taken of her, one majestic morning on the banks of the Rhine. She looked so beautiful. He remembered the sun as it hit her just enough to make her glow. Looking over at the very few photos and tangible memories of his family and youth he began to reminisce of about own family and younger life.

Looking at a black-and-white creased photo of his two parents, Henry remembered growing up happy. Poor, but happy. His parents worked hard for him, working the land, and operating a small farm. They sold corn and apples, as well as eggs and milk, doing their best to provide the food and shelter he and his siblings needed. As Henry grew older, it was becoming apparent that he was the smartest in the family, and desired to get into the medical field. Without any regrets, Henry's parents planted more crops, took in more animals, worked longer hours and did whatever they needed to do to find the resources to send Henry to university. Luckily Henry had the work ethic of his parents and with studying full time, working part time, and with a large percentage of the schooling free, Henry was able to complete his education at the top of his class. Henry was driven. He was the type of person that once he found his path, he did whatever was necessary to complete the path, with little getting in his way. Looking back at the photo of Carmen, Henry realized that in matters of love, though, he found it a bit more difficult, but he was okay with that. Henry smiled looking at the photo of his beautiful bride, knowing the anxiety and stress she caused him as she had flirted with him all those years ago.

His brother and sister didn't fare so well, unfortunately. Henry had been only in his second year of his schooling when both of them passed away from polio. He was the middle child, and losing both an older and a younger sibling, not to mention all of his siblings, was hard on him. It was a tough time for Henry and his parents, but having Carmen around, even though they were still only dating, made things a little more bearable. *"Different times then,"* he thought, even if they were somehow difficult in their own way. But that was yesterday and now is today, and there wasn't much to do about it.

A few minutes into his routine that consisted of, in part, morning dusting, his phone rang.

"Hello?" asked Henry in his native tongue.

"Is this Dr. Henry Meier?" asked the strange male voice, in the same language.

"It is. How may I help you?"

"This is Lieutenant Schmidt. We have taken some casualties just north of your position and require your assistance again." demanded the lieutenant.

"How many?" wondered Henry out loud.

"At least thirty men, doctor. We will be at your coordinates at 1300hrs."

"How…how come you're so close. I haven't heard or seen much of the army for at least six months now?" stammered Henry, trying to get some information as the lieutenant tried to hang up.

"Not going well, Doctor," replied the ranking soldier. "1300hrs. be ready for us."

Henry slid the phone down from his ear and placed it gently on the receiver. Taking a deep breath, he eased himself into the cracked leather chair at his desk. "Not again," he mumbled. "I can't risk being involved again." The worried Doctor looked out of his dusty window into the farmyards, which lined the hills in the distance, and found it hard to believe that Hitler's troops were so close to him now. He would need Carmen again. He couldn't do this without her, he knew. She would hate this, of course, but eventually she would understand that ultimately, they had to save lives, even if those lives were being wasted. Considering what it could cost them if they didn't help was almost as good an incentive. Henry knew too well the reward of helping may be small or even never come to fruition, but the cost of not helping could be devastating. The German army didn't take lightly those that refused to serve, in whatever capacity they demanded of you.

"Carmen!" Henry called from the staircase as he approached his apartment. They didn't have a phone so he had rushed over to talk to her. In fact, the only reason he had one at his office now, was for the very reason he was called that morning.

"Carmen." He called again, as he opened the door.

"What is it, Henry?" Carmen asked, putting on a robe as she gently closed the door to their bedroom, hoping their daughter wouldn't awake so early.

"I need you at the office as soon as you can."

"Why, what's wrong"

Henry stared back and paused.

"Henry, no." Carmen responded before he could. "How many?"

"At least a few dozen, I'm not really sure. I'm going to have to clear out the basement of the bakery again, but I don't know if we have enough supplies this time." Henry trailed off, making preparations in his mind already.

"Off then. I'll ask Maria next door to come over and I'll get down there as soon as I can."

Before Henry could say anything, Carmen was closing the door on him, and starting to remove her gown. He loved her for that. Even in these terrible times, with the war now seemingly on their doorstep, she didn't skip a beat, and got right down to business. He turned, heading down the stairs, when the apartment door cracked open again, Carmen's face poking through.

"Be careful Henry," she insisted. "We barely avoided it the first time."

With a sad smile, she closed the door again and left Henry to tromp down the stairs and return to his office, making preparations for more wounded than his little office could handle.

Grass, soil and muck careened into the air, a split second after the mortar hit the once green and lush field. One after another, bombs that flew with less-than-accurate precision landed within metres of the trenches, lifting massive amounts of sand and dirt into the air. The muck cascaded in all directions, spreading it around more efficiently than any gardener could. Wooden planks that held the trench together buckled and crumbled under the massive amount of force determined to enter the vacant space. The aroma of death and gunpowder clung to the air.

A young Canadian soldier wiped away mud from his already caked face, as it sprayed across him much like the ocean mist did at home. He hadn't seen much action in days, but this was more than he had seen since arriving over two months ago. Raising the muzzle of his gun over the lip of the trench he tried to peer into the fog in front of him, desperately wanting to find an enemy soldier to eliminate. He pressed into his trigger just enough so that once the command was given, his gun would fire immediately. His heart felt like it could bust out of his chest at any moment. Even with the lack of sleep, his mind and body were wide awake and alert. His commanding officer flew from position to position, trying to gauge how many of his forces still stood alive within their trench.

"Malloy, Johnson, Beedie!" he yelled.

Everyone looked back and forth, glad that their names hadn't been called, but curious whether the names would answer back. The Germans had planned this one out well; with minimal men at their disposal, they had waited for days. They waited for the English to grow weary, and to think that their current position was secured. The Germans remained silently in place, until very early in the morning when the fog obscured most of the large field separating the two platoons. They had crawled silently out onto the wet grass a few dozen strong, and had set up small mortar launchers and took aim as best as they could. Their goal would be simple, catch the English in surprise, and blast the hell out of them.

Kaboom!

Another mortar landed only a few feet behind the young Canadian, creating a small mudslide to his left. Watching the mud drift into the trench, he caught sight of the feet and legs of a soldier that drifted with it. He didn't see any more parts of it. Shuffling over to his right, he plowed into the soldier next to him, avoiding more of the mud that still rushed in to fill whatever space it could.

"Alan!" the neighboring soldier called, feeling the warm body plunge into him. He had been concentrating so hard on the enemy in front, he hadn't even noticed the destruction beside him. "Are you all right?"

Alan looked at him and smiled, faced covered in mud better than any helmet could.

"I'm all right," Alan responded, breathing deeply.

"What do you think he's doing?" Alan's companion asked, staring at their superior officer still calling out more names.

"Not sure, has he called you?"

"No John yet, thankfully."

John was Alan's best friend. At least he has been, since they've been over here. He was his girlfriend's brother, after all, so they had always been friends since they met, but the war had brought them much closer than they would have ever been, living at home. They felt more like brothers than friends. It was a bond that they relied on, something that both of them could count on when times were rough.

"Doesn't look good, does it?" John continued, returning his gaze to the sandbags and wooden planks that made up the sides of their trench.

Alan looked farther to his right, to see a group of English soldiers creep over the wall as silently and quickly as they could.

"Looks like they're going over to take care of the Germans." Alan surmised. "I guess with the fog they've got somewhat of a chance."

"If they make it there alive."

John shook his head, seeing only more death ahead. Both Alan and John peeked over the wall as best as they could through the thick fog, trying to find out what was going on, but found only wet mist.

Both looked up as the familiar whistle of a bomb grew louder and louder. The awful sound grew lower in pitch with every second on its way to its target.

John turned to Alan, his face ashen.

"Get down!" he screamed as loud as he could, pushing Alan hard, back to where the mud slowly collected on the trench floor. Alan tripped over a root in the dirt and toppled face-first in the mud, feeling the cold wet dirt wash over his face. Even under the thin layer of mud his ears rung, sending his mind to a different place, a place of confusion and terror. The shock of the blast silenced everything around him. The war fell silent, slowing to a perceived stop-motion, as the bomb landed against the far wall of the trench a dozen feet from his best friend, John.

Alan closed his eyes tight, feeling the ringing in his ears begin to make him nauseous. He could barely breathe and lifted himself out of the mud, discarding his rifle in the process.

"John!" Alan called out barely hearing his own words. "John!" he called again, unable to realize that he wouldn't be able to hear him if he tried.

After a few seconds, Alan opened his eyes to Hell. Or at least he tried. Squinting through the blur in his vision made him even more nauseous. He tried to focus on what was in front of him, but he remained in place, trying as hard as he could to stop his eyes from giving him an awful dizzy picture. Looking at his hands in front of him, he could see the picture slowly come into focus. Dirt, sweat, blood and tears soaked his hands, then his pants, and then everything around him. He finally looked up into the distance and could finally realize the horror that fell upon him. The trench had been blown open. Wood, sand, and dirt were scattered everywhere. The foggy field in front was clearly visible up the sides of the crater. Alan looked around to find John, praying hard that he was still alive. Instinct made him grab hold of his friend's arm and face, and check for a pulse, or for any signs of life. He did not immediately realize that his friend's body wasn't even in one piece. When he glanced away from his friend's head and torso, what pieces he did see told him all that he needed to know. That realization came as his training set back in, and his breathing calmed down enough to focus on his surroundings properly. Tears streamed down his filthy cheeks, creating small dirty, salty rivers that flowed freely down his face.

The Canadian soldier looked up to the heavens in desperation searching for a meaning. It was only a minute when he realized the mortar attack had stopped. The English counter had proved successful. "Little help now," Alan muttered crying for his best friend. What would he tell Lizzy? How could he tell her that her brother was dead?

Chapter Two

He knew what she had meant of course, as he opened up all of his cabinet drawers, emptying them of supplies into large containers on the floor. It was shortly after he had opened his office when the call came in. A skirmish had broken out, not 15 kilometres away, and he would have to pack up his bags and help out with the wounded. It would be his first time this close to the front line.

He was still finishing his studies when the war had broken out, and the army had allowed him to finish instead of being drafted. Either finish his studies, with the Army waiting patiently in order to draft him as a medic, or get drafted immediately and fight as a common soldier. Neither seemed to offer much in the way of a happy future, but at least he could become a doctor, and at the Government's expense at that. Finally receiving his medical degree, he had thought he was all but forgotten until someone contacted him shortly after he had moved here and started up his own practice. Unfortunately, it seemed as if someone who had lived here had remembered him from this town and knew that he had opened up shop not far from their current position.

Henry shuddered remembering those days spent up on the hill in a long narrow bunker, administering what little help he could, to those that were fighting as much for their lives as for their cause. Looking down at his uniform, it had hung from his body as it would hang from a manikin in a second hand store. It didn't feel like part of him, it didn't look like part of him, and only the demand on his services kept him focused enough to complete each day. He had shuddered thinking of what he had become, and how little a choice he was given. It seemed pointless patching up wounds that would only enable the soldier to get back into the fray, eventually coming out of it in a body bag.

"I'm going to die, aren't I?" cried one young soldier. Henry didn't even know his name.

"No, you're not! You're going to be okay. You'll be home soon, don't worry." Henry had lied the best that he could, watching the blood pour out of the soldier's back and stomach. Even morphine was at a premium, and all he could do was stare into the man's eyes and offer what little comfort he could give, as the life slipped away from him. He hadn't the supplies available to comfort him properly in the last moments of his life. Henry sighed looking into the face of the soldier, praying that his words and presence gave him some measure of comfort. Death finally overtook him, for whatever little satisfaction that gave. The platoon had won that skirmish, however. And with yells and cheers, the officers gathered up the troops and signaled that they would be picking up stakes and heading north to meet up with another regiment.

Shaking his head, Henry grabbed the large box of supplies and made his way next door to the abandoned bakery. There was a large supply room in the basement that had served this purpose before, and unfortunately it would have to serve again. Old worn cots and blankets were still stored there, along with some rusty surgical supplies that lay in a pile by the door. He had desperately hoped that he would never have to see this place again, or at least not in this capacity.

He was an hour into sweeping and dusting as best he could when Carmen opened the door and surveyed the situation. "What's next?" Carmen demanded, ready to get on with the business of saving lives. "Still need to organize the beds, and we need to at least try to sterilize some of the equipment," Henry responded. "I'll get the stove going and boil some water," his nurse stated, as she headed to the small iron stove in the corner of the room. "Grab me as many utensils as you have and we'll do our best." Doctor and nurse, husband and wife, they worked as hard and as fast as they could getting ready for the inevitable. Minutes dragged and sweat poured as the supply room took the form of a triage centre.

Another hour had gone by, when Carmen perked up her head and strained to listen through the small window high in the room.

"Shh, I hear something."

Henry stopped, along with his heart. Each craned their ears, wondering if this was the sound that they were dreading. Seconds ticked by. Nothing. A bead of sweat slowly dripped down from Henry's brow, sliding down his crooked nose, collecting in a droplet on the tip, finally dropping to the floor below.

"There!" Carmen pointed.

Sure enough, he could hear the sounds of German jeeps muscling their way into the small town, bouncing on the unkempt concrete road. Within minutes, wounded were being dragged, pulled and carried down the open staircase into the makeshift hospital. Henry paused for a brief moment, feeling that same horror he had felt back in the trenches not so long ago. *"No time to think,"* Henry ironically thought to himself.

The next hours were but a blur to both Henry and Carmen. Details were vivid and then faded as they passed from patient to patient. Henry would assess each one as fast as he could, giving those that needed the least attention a spot in the far corner. Those that required more immediate care, but could be handled by Carmen, were passed off. Even more disturbing were those that Henry felt that were beyond his expertise, or required more than his small equipment supplies could handle. He merely gave one saddened glance to the soldier, then one to an officer or a friend, who stood by, and moved on. "Am I going to die!?" cried one such soldier to Henry, who had heard that tragic call before. "I'm going to die aren't' I! Please doctor, I don't want to die!"

His pain was beyond him, and he strained to look at his hands, which were holding his intestines loosely in place. His glazed eyes searched Henry for some comfort. "My children." he muttered almost incoherently, "I'll never see them again."

Henry had few more tears to offer, but found one more, which slid slowly down his cheek. He grabbed the soldier's bloody hand, and stared into his eyes. "You'll be all right, son," he lied. "You'll see your children soon, don't worry." Henry was right in a sense, but that seemed not to make a difference now. He held the young man's hand until its grip loosened and then let go. His face lightened up, and he smiled as death overtook him. *This is about the best I've done so far.* Henry thought sarcastically. Before he could even close the soldier's eyes, another shout came from a cot across the room.

"Doctor! Hurry! He's dying!"

Henry could hardly think anymore. Shouting came from everywhere. Everyone was dying. Everyone needed him. He moved on instinct, bouncing from patient to patient, administering what he could, the best he could, calling on his trusted nurse and wife when he was finished, for her to sew up the injury or to clean a wound.

Blood pooled on the floor. Like a red shagged carpet, it rippled as he walked across it. The constant moaning and yelling rattled inside his ears. More and more injured were led down to the makeshift triage room. Those that had no chance were unfortunately roughly dragged outside to lie down beside the others that weren't so fortunate, in order to speed the process for those who might be saved. Those that were done being treated and could be moved were taken upstairs to rest as best as they could. Looking back, Henry would admit that this was his finest day as a doctor. He flew through the room patching and repairing. Bullets were dislodged and pried loose; bones were set with amazing speed. He rarely said a word in the hours that followed, only calling for his wife regularly, and yelling at the odd soldier to hurry up and remove someone or bring another victim to a bed to be treated.

"I've got a bleeder over here!" screamed Carmen.

Henry kicked a discarded helmet across the floor, as he rushed over to a young corporal, whose leg took the form of a fountain. Thick red blood gushed out of an artery and Carmen was trying her best to hold in as much of it as she could. His leg was smashed beyond repair. "What a mess," Henry remarked under his breath. A lieutenant stood nearby, looked desperately at Henry, hearing his distressed voice. "Please, sir. Save him." He looked down at the soldier with obvious concern. His rank and power dissipated now, filled only with worry for his patient. "He's my son."

Henry looked at him ever so briefly, and then focused his attention to the injury. With a quick assessment, he glanced at his wife. "We can't save his leg." Henry whispered as quietly as he could over the noise in the room. He shot a quick glance at the father who craned to hear as much as he could. "He is losing blood too fast. We need to amputate now, or we lose him too."

Carmen again rose to the challenge. She leapt from the side of the bed to a tray of tools standing nearby. Blood gushed with renewed vigor as Henry quickly ripped a piece of cloth from the bed linen and began to tie a tourniquet around the soldier. With a hushed grunt, Henry knotted the strip of linen tightly as the blood slowed to a small trickle. Carmen returned with the proper surgical equipment, and immediately handed over a large toothed saw to her husband.

Just before placing the saw onto his leg, Henry called to the lieutenant. "Over to the stove, there's a piece of iron sitting in the fire." The father looked to the far side of the room.

"Go get it, Henry demanded. "Now!"

Partly out of pity, partly out of necessity, he sent the discouraged soldier to retrieve the iron, which would cauterize the wound. "Nothing for it," Henry muttered, as was his favorite expression in better times. With a quick clean stroke, he drew the saw through most of the mutilated leg. Blood now spread out on all sides in a slow pulsing mess. With a slight pause, the saw came back towards

Henry, taking off the leg completely above the knee, through the thigh. Carmen grabbed the bodiless limb and threw it on an empty cart, and then threw a piece of tarp over top. The lieutenant jogged back, looking with astonishment at his son, and handing over the red-hot iron to Henry, who grasped it carefully at the cooler end.

"Stand back."

Henry placed the iron firmly against the exposed area and a ball of hot steam sprouted forth. The smell singed Henry's nose, which even after all these years made him feel nauseous. Henry pulled back for a second, and then one more time placed the iron over the exposed flesh. Once again steam lifted into the air, though not as high or as dense. Any blood that had oozed out stopped, and the doctor with amazed precision collapsed remaining skin around the wound, and began to sew it up.

"Lieutenant!" a voice called from the back of the room, and then paused.

"Lieutenant!"

The protective father awoke from his paternal gaze and lifted his eyes to see where the voice was coming from. When their eyes met, he nodded firmly.

"I have to go. Please take care of him, doctor," he asked, sounding less like an order and more of a request.

The lieutenant strode away to the back of the triage centre, past the beds of his soldiers who lay awaiting their fate.

Henry glanced at Carmen, and both realized that he must be the one in charge, or at least the highest-ranking officer still alive.

"Can you handle the rest?" questioned Henry.

"Go. Take care of the others," demanded the capable nurse. "I'll finish up here and make sure that he will be all right."

Henry sighed as he looked to where he was needed the most, and again his mind drifted to better times, as his abilities took over.

It was several hours later that the noise and confusion diminished to a dull hum. No more patients came in, and a slow but steady stream of bodies and recovering soldiers were being taken up the stairs to the outside. Henry surveyed the room, seeing all but a few who still couldn't be moved, yet nothing more could be done to help. Carmen was still making her last patches and mends, inserting an IV tube into one, and placing a sling on another. He glanced out the small window. It was nighttime already. He never even realized it until now. He also felt sweat line his body, making his gown cling to him as if he had just taken a swim. It was hot. With temperatures outside still cool, the fire inside still burning hot, he felt his body finally absorb the effects of this day.

Henry called an able-bodied soldier over, and ordered him to extinguish the fire in the stove and have him make sure there were no more victims left to come in.

"Yes sir," replied the teenage trooper, who looked at the doctor with strange cold eyes, not liking the fact he was taking orders from a civilian.

As he stood where he was, taking deep breaths, Carmen walked over wiping some of the blood off her arms with a blood-soaked cloth.

"You look tired," Henry remarked lovingly. "Look at you, doctor," smiled Carmen, while holding his gaze.

"Go home," Henry replied. "I can handle the rest here. It's late and you need to rest. Eden will be up in a few hours, and I'm sure Maria will be glad to see you."

Carmen continued to stare at her beloved husband, not sure if she should protest or not, knowing that he was right. She was tired, and Eden would not like to be woken up in a strange place.

"I'll see you in a while, honey. Just a few more rounds, and there is little more we can do tonight." Henry continued, seeing the agreement in her eyes.

"Come soon then."

With a childlike kiss to the cheek, Carmen gingerly stepped to the stairs, avoiding the pools of blood and blood-soaked rags that littered the ground. She continued without a pause through the door and out into the street above.

Chapter Three

With another deep breath, Henry walked to the opposite end of the storage room, scanning each remaining patient and making sure that there was indeed nothing more to be done in the short term. Satisfied, he continued up the opposing staircase that led to the rear of the bakery, where he was curious to see to what disarray the army was in.

To his amazement, things looked to be in almost complete order. A few large green tents were erected on the grass, and soldiers were lined up neatly in rows along each side. Those that had entered whatever afterlife they believe in were placed beside each other, with tarps and blankets covering their faces for what little dignity could be offered. The more severely wounded were being looked after by appointed medics, who were tried to comfort them and ease their pain as best as they could. Others were already sitting up, and talking to each other in hushed tones, glad that they had come away alive from this one. Activity was noticeable from a smaller tent set up toward the left. Even with the night almost giving itself over to another day, higher ranked soldiers discussed plans that seemed important, with the aid of a large map that kept the conversation heated. One pointed to one end of the map, while another pointed somewhere else.

Henry was glad that he hadn't been forced to enter the silly game of war, at least not on the killing side. It seemed so useless. Fighting for a cause he figured that was unknown, not understood, and most often, not important. To pledge your life for a man that didn't know your name seemed to be a great shame. Henry caught the eye of a soldier who hobbled on makeshift crutches to the edge of the compound to light a smoke. He looked into Henry's eyes with what thanks he could muster. He knew that Henry had saved him, maybe not from death this time, but certainly from further pain and permanent discomfort. He also knew that every day brought the possibility of another disaster. Henry wrenched his eyes away from him, as the realization hit him that this young soldier hadn't pledged his life. He hadn't volunteered for service for his country. He was an unwilling boy ordered into a man's war. He could see it in his eyes. Henry shuddered to think how lucky he was.

With his bloody gown starting to smell and stain, Henry caught the silhouette of the lieutenant looking over the body of his son in another small tent to his right, both glowing softly from the randomly placed lanterns and the soft pale moonlight. As if feeling his gaze, the man in charge glanced back at him and ushered him over. With slow uneasy steps, Henry stepped toward him.

"There is not much else I can do tonight sir," Henry revealed, as if compelled to give him an update.

"You've done lots, doctor."

The lieutenant turned toward his son, who lay on a small cot, his face slightly pale but in peace. His stomach rose and fell with deep breaths, catching up on what his body desperately needed.

"I can't thank you enough for saving him."

"I'm sorry about his leg. There really was nothing I co–"

"I know. I know," he interrupted kindly. "I'm just glad to have him. He'll go home now, back to his mother. I just hope there is still a home to go back to."

Henry looked up into his face, seeing the disillusion that war had traced upon it.

"It's not going well, you know," he continued. "It seems we're constantly in retreat now. We won't be safe here, either, for long."

Henry's heart skipped a beat.

"There will be more injuries to come. More casualties of war, I'm afraid. We could certainly use someone of your expertise in the days ahead."

Henry's heart skipped once again, and then stopped. It felt like it fell to the floor with the thud. He couldn't move. His eyes locked on the other man, who turned away.

A few seconds of silence fell away, and the lieutenant turned again to meet Henry's eyes, and seeing him grow paler by the second, understood the horror that lived there.

"You don't want to serve your country in this war, do you?" The lieutenant questioned.

"It's…it's not that I don't want to serve my country, you know. I just…just don't think I could offer much," Henry attempted.

"Don't be so modest, doctor. I saw your skills today. You would be most welcome, you know."

Henry opened his mouth, as if to reply. He couldn't form a train of thought, couldn't even begin to put a sentence together in response.

"I know you, you know," he continued. "I was there, that time up on the hill. It seems a long time ago now."

Henry's eyes furrowed in thought.

"I was a corporal, back then. I came away untouched that day, but I saw what you did to those boys. You risked your life to help our guys. I even know of your conversation with the General."

Henry's face lightened suddenly, recollection of that day coming to the forefront of his mind.

"I know how he saw the same thing that I did. He was very impressed with you."

The former corporal looked to the horizon, realizing what he was about to do.

"The war was different back then, you know." Herr Schmidt turned his gaze back to Henry. "Things aren't as upbeat as they were. We are constantly on the run, losing ground in every confrontation. It's utterly frustrating!"

Henry watched as the lieutenant's face reddened and the anger swelled up inside.

"We keep asking for reinforcements, but they just don't come. They don't seem to care that we're all dying down here."

He took another glance at his son lying beside him breathing deeply.

Henry felt uneasy listening to the commanding officer grow less polite and more commanding. Henry felt trapped, not sure of what he was doing there, and yet sure that whatever came next wouldn't be good.

"I need you, doctor," the lieutenant ordered with a hint of an apology.

Henry's heart finally stopped and dropped. He had dreaded hearing those words for many years. His thoughts concentrated on his wife and child. They would be devastated. Their worst fears realized. It was a death sentence to be sure. If what the lieutenant said were true, the war would no longer be in Germany's favour.

He couldn't leave his family. Not now. Not after all they have lived through.

Henry's thoughts were cut off, as the lieutenant took a deep breath and faced Henry squarely.

"As commanding officer of this regiment, I'm ordering you to serve your country and enlist you as chief medical officer for this region. We will be shipping out by 0900 hours tomorrow morning. We are heading south to meet with what is left of the 2nd battalion, who are stationed fifty miles south of here, trying to take back a bridge on the Rhine."

"But…but…,"Henry stammered. "I thought that I was…"

"You were given reprieve from the war, I know." The commanding officer interrupted. "But I am rescinding that order. I have been given all authority to enlist however and whomever I need as I see fit, and I know there will be more casualties ahead, and someone of your calling will be invaluable."

"What about all those injured here? Surely you don't expect them to get up and march out of here in such a short period of time." Henry gestured to those bodies lying all around them.

"What about your son? I could take better care of him here."

Lieutenant Schmidt looked briefly to the sky, and then back to Henry. "Those that can walk will walk, and those that can't, will be left here with what provisions can be spared." The lieutenant said it so calmly, Henry thought he was joking.

"But they won't survive long on their own. Who will take care of them? You saved them, just to let them die in the cold air?" Henry voiced stammered as he desperately tried to change the man's mind.

"They will be better off than us, doctor. They'll be found soon enough, and receive better care than we can offer."

"And your son?" Henry pressed.

Again, the father sighed and looked to his injured son lying on the small cot.

"Him too. At least I know someone will be taking care of him."

"But…but I can do that here, in my office," Henry stammered.

The lieutenant swung back to the doctor quickly. "Enough, doctor! Don't you understand? This town will be overrun with English in a few days. They will take care of him, and when the war is over, maybe I'll get to see him one more time."

Henry breathed heavily, realizing that he would be unable to convince him otherwise.

"Say good-bye to your family and be ready to leave at 0900 hours." Lieutenant Schmidt placed his hand over the revolver at his hip. "Don't think otherwise."

Henry staggered to his apartment, torn between wanting to run into his lover's arms and wanting to hide somewhere praying for this all to be a bad dream. He took off his bloody smock, letting it slide off his arms, hanging it on the first post of the staircase, as he climbed them step by step, dreading the sight of his wife when he would tell her their lives would change forever. He opened the front door of the apartment to find Carmen putting together what little food they had in the kitchen, in preparation of her husband's return. She turned toward the door with a broad smile, which quickly fell away as she saw what little joy lived in Henry's face. Instinctively she knew what had happened.

"Oh Henry!" Carmen gasped. "No. Please no."

"I leave first thing tomorrow morning." Henry didn't even try to sugarcoat the fact that he would be involuntarily enlisting in the army. She deserved the straight truth, as she was smart enough to figure it out anyway.

Carmen's voice quivered. "But you were told you didn't have to serve, that you would be more helpful where you were."

"Apparently, that doesn't matter anymore," Henry replied quickly. "He feels that the war has changed and I'm needed."

Carmen stared at her husband, and after a few seconds, turned to their daughter, handing her a spoon in order for her to feed herself. She immediately made her way to the small closet near the door and retrieved a suitcase that sat on top of the two or three coats inside.

"We'll just have to leave then."

Henry shook his head slowly.

"I'll pack up some things and we'll all hide somewhere. Somewhere they can't find us."

"Where, Carmen?" Henry raised his voice slightly. "Where are we supposed to hide?"

"I don't know. I don't care. We'll do whatever it takes. We'll run wherever we have to."

"Carmen." Henry cut her short. "Run? With Eden in tow? In a country at war? I can't risk her like that. We wouldn't survive."

"I don't care," Carmen replied defensively. "I just don't care. They can't take you away from us. They can't. I won't let them."

"You'll be safe here, without me, without the German army lingering here. Where I am to go, you know you won't be safe." A tear forming in his eye, just enough to make Carmen pause with understanding.

Carmen dropped the suitcase to the floor and put her hand to her face as tears welled up in her eyes. Henry came close as Carmen lost strength in her legs and leaned heavily on her husband. Eden, who still held the small spoon in her hand, began to cry, sensing the desperation in the air.

Henry dragged Carmen to the kitchen table, and with outstretched arm grasped Eden, holding each of them as hard as he could, his own tears sliding down his cheek.

"Sir?" the corporal asked gingerly.

Lieutenant Schmidt, turned to meet the young officer at the edge of the camp, where he was in deep thought.

"Yes, Corporal."

"News from the scouts you sent out."

A moment's silence cut through the air as the corporal awaited a response from his head in command.

"Out with it then, corporal," Schmidt demanded, irritated.

"They…well. They report activity from the English about ten miles south."

"Oh, my." Schmidt sighed worriedly. "What kind of activity?"

"Troop movement, I think."

"You think?"

"Some English in uniform were spotted, I mean. A few English patrols were seen." The young man tried to spit out his information as quickly as he could, "Do you think they know we're here?"

"They know all right." The lieutenant admitted. "They know. Wake the troops. Have everyone that can march, ready to go within the hour."

Lieutenant Schmidt arched his back, stretching his back tight after a long day and night.

"And have someone get the doctor at his apartment. He's coming with us!" he shouted at the corporal as he was running away.

The young man turned as he heard Schmidt shout, and nodded, turning back toward the main camp.

Chapter Four

Henry woke quickly with the premonition of something that has gone amiss. His wife and child were still holding on to each other, lying on the sofa. Henry scanned the window to notice the darkness was giving its way to the impending sunlight. Who knew what this day would bring?

Knock. Knock.

Henry's heart stopped as he looked at the door. Looking down at his family, his wife with her head on his lap and their child in her arms, he sighed in relief, as they stirred slightly but remained asleep. He didn't want to answer the door, knowing it could be nothing but worse news, but realized he really had no option but to slide out from under Carmen's head and walk to the door. Scanning the clock that sat on the mantle, he realized that he could have only been sleeping for a few hours.

Henry unlocked the door slowly, opening it to find a young man, armed and very unnerved.

"You…you need to come with me right away, sir." The young soldier stated.

"Not yet." The doctor responded. "I was told 0900 hours, and I haven't packed yet."

Henry placed his hand on the door as if to signal he wished to close it.

"Sorry sir, no time. I have orders to escort you to the main camp, ASAP."

"All right then, but let me get my things together and I'll be there in a minute."

Henry started to close the door on the soldier, but before he got it to move an inch, the barrel of the young man's rifle thudded on the door, not allowing it to move any further.

"Now, doctor," the soldier tried his hardest to sound inflexible. "We go now."

Henry looked back to his family lying peacefully together, and with a tear in his eye turned to the door and walked through, changing his life forever.

Henry grabbed his dirty smock from the post where he had left it only a few hours before, somehow feeling the need of it. With the soldier following a few steps behind him, Henry opened the door that led to the street out front. Taking a few steps on the pavement, Henry spotted from the corner of his eye a figure dashing between two buildings. He stopped and turned back to see if his escort had seen something, and from the look of him, he certainly had.

"Don't stop, doctor." The soldier quivered, "Hurry."

Henry felt the tip of the rifle press into his back, and with no argument continued to walk across the street, his eyes darting back and forth wondering if what he thought was happening was indeed really happening.

Just as he reached the far end of the street, turning to his left in order to make his way back to the old bakery, Henry spotted another figure standing just inside a doorway. It was positioned in such a way that it would be the doctor who would see him first as they walked along. Two things became immediately obvious. One was that this figure was not a German soldier, and the other was that he was trying to get Henry's attention. Henry cocked his head as the soldier in the doorway motioned for him to get on the ground. Seconds ticked away as if they were minutes, as the soldier once more waved his hand down hard, in order for Henry to get his message. Henry glanced back once more at his young armed escort, seeing his eyes dart back and forth in obvious terror, sensing trouble was coming, but not knowing when and where it would come from. His face was white as a ghost, clutching his rifle as if someone would rip it from his grip. Henry turned again to the English soldier in the doorway, noticing that man's own rifle now pointing directly at him. In an instant, Henry realized what was happening and dropped to the ground as fire exploded from the end of the barrel. The familiar bang of a gun was deadened from an unfamiliar-looking silencer placed at the end of the rifle. From behind his head, Henry heard a thud and a grunt, followed by the lifeless body of the German soldier falling to the ground behind him. Looking at the figure across the street, he could almost sense a smile cross the soldiers face. Henry had but a second to again look behind him, seeing the all too familiar rich red liquid pool behind the young man's head, before rough arms grabbed him and yanked him up to his feet.

"Civilian?" demanded the soldier, in English.

Henry nodded, having an excellent grasp of the English language, learning it in both grade school and university.

"Follow me," the soldier commanded.

With quick steps, the pair walked in the opposite direction of the makeshift German camp. The English man scanned the area as they hurriedly walked to a small park, which sat in the east section of town. Awaiting them were a few more soldiers, who were apparently guarding other civilians liberated from town.

"Hold him here with the rest, corporal." Henry's saviour ordered, pointing toward the small group that already sat dumbfounded on the lawn.

After receiving a nod from the other soldier, the large English soldier turned toward town with rifle in hand.

"What's happening?" Henry called to him, in his learned English.

As he turned back, Henry noticed a red and white patch on the man's army uniform, on his shoulder, which he seemed to remember belonged to a country near America. Canadian, he figured, if his high school geography memory was correct.

"We're here to liberate you."

Without waiting for a response, the Canadian soldier jogged back in the direction of the German army camp, rifle held ready. Minutes dragged on as Henry sat with a few of his fellow townspeople in the quiet park. The air was eerily without noise, and only the occasional bird chirping from the treetop above broke the silence.

Henry's heart beat steadily and his face began to grow moist as sweat formed on his brow. His hands still shook, desperately looking in the direction of his home, fearful for his family. Looking around, he saw desperation on each of the others' faces. He thought he should say something, but there really was nothing to say. He couldn't stay still, thinking of his family lying in their apartment unaware of the danger that approached. He wasn't fond of the German Army, to say the least. and he had always dreamed that one day the English would come and put an end to all of the madness, but with that came more war, and more casualties.

A squawk of a radio cut through the silence. Henry spun around to see the young corporal remove the receiver of a large radio sitting on the ground.

"Yes, sir," the boy replied to the voice from the box. "Yes, sir."

With another acknowledgment, the young man replaced the receiver and cracked a smile.

"It starts now, folks."

A single shot echoed through the air, its sound rebounding off the few small buildings in the area. Immediately it was followed by the scream of a soon-to-be lifeless victim. Everyone dropped to the ground, unsure what else to do, how else to be safe. A split second later it indeed started. The noise of gunfire cracked the air in a volley. Seconds, and then minutes raced by as the gunfire could be heard from the town. An old woman who sat uncomfortably in the grass, tried her best to plug her ears, as tears raced down her face.

Henry couldn't stand it any longer. Carmen would surely hear everything now. Eden would be screaming in fear. With a surge of adrenaline and confidence, but mostly of desperation, Henry stood up wiping the sweat from his forehead, and took a step in the direction of death.

He barely got one step before a shout came from behind him.

"Stop right there!"

Henry turned in mid-stride to see the cocky soldier, with rifle pointed, looking at him.

"But, but my family. My wife and daughter..." Henry pleaded in his best English. "They are all alone, there."

"Sorry sir. I can't allow it."

"Please, sir. I have to go to them."

Tears welled up in his eyes, thinking of them alone in their small apartment.

"You seem like a decent man," replied the soldier. "A doctor it looks like," the soldier noticed the smock and some basic physician tools that the German man wore. "But I can't risk it."

The rifle still pointed at his chest, Henry stood in place, unsure of what to do. Emotions drove him to take another step. The rifle cocked.

"I *will* shoot." The soldier paused to gauge Henry's determined stance. "I don't want to, but I will."

Henry continued to stand; now facing the direction of his home, and the continued gunfire. Putting his hands over his face, he collapsed to the floor, his mind unable to focus on anything besides fear.

Within the town, soldiers were braced in combat. What was left of the German army remained huddled near their own injured, crouching behind trees and sandbags. Schmidt yelled at a tall soldier who hunched himself over as best he could behind an old apple tree ten metres away. Catching his attention, Schmidt motioned to him to grab the radio from his back and call for help. He figured the 2nd Battalion would be days away, but maybe there would be some cut-off troops somewhere nearby. He desperately hoped. He couldn't hold the English for long, but maybe a day, just maybe just a day.

Turning back to the opposing gunfire, he knew they couldn't hold up here for very long. Hoping to draw the English away from the wounded, he ordered half of his men to seek refuge in the abandoned bakery, and the other half to attempt to flank the English to the west. With a glance at the tent, which covered his son, Schmidt grabbed his rifle and dove the few metres across the clearing to the stairwell into the basement.

The day grew long as the fighting continued. Henry and the others remained huddled on the grass, saying few words. Gunfire persisted, but not as fervently as it had started. The odd shot echoed through the town, making Henry shudder each time. It seemed as if the initial surprise was over, and now the figurative game of chess began. Each side was now finding their best points of attack, engaging each other when the chance presented itself. Neither side seemed willing to risk taking the offensive; neither also seemed to understand exactly why the other wouldn't.

Hunger had crept up on Henry throughout the day, finally hitting him with a gut-wrenching thud. It didn't seem fair to think about food right now, but thinking back, he couldn't remember the last time he had eaten anything substantial. "Do you have anything to eat?" he asked the group of soldiers that had now set up a mini base in the park.

One soldier turned to him and then talked softly to another sitting close by.

"Be patient, sir. Food will come soon," replied the second soldier.

Henry nodded his head in agreement, and noticed how polite these Canadian soldiers were.

True to his promise, supplies started arriving within an hour. Boxes of food and ammunition unloaded from a truck were piled inside the clearing. Sandbags had been made to encircle the small group of townspeople, housing a rather large machine gun, and around ten or so soldiers. A few small tents were erected, and the original corporal who had been there since the beginning seemed to be in charge, giving commands to the others.

Eventually, buns and cold soup were brought to the group of hungry Germans, who gladly accepted them and sat in silence devouring whatever they were given.

As they sat eating, darkness again started to crawl back, hiding the light. Henry prayed continually that Carmen and Eden were safe, hoping they remained in their apartment, and moreover that no one entered. He was almost certain that Maria would be with them by now, which gave him some small comfort.

As the gunfire seemed to lessen each hour, Henry heard a low rumbling noise from in the distance. He couldn't put his finger on it, but the picture of a large vehicle formed in his mind. His skin twitched, and tingled.

He hated the sounds of war, he thought. He hated it.

Turning his attention to his cold soup, Henry's thoughts drifted to how much more food was available to be eaten.

Once again, the crackle of the army radio cut through the morning air. A soldier, who sported a long thin moustache, handed the receiver to the man in charge.

"Headquarters, sir!"

"Thank you soldier," the corporal replied methodically.

He listened to the receiver for a brief moment, nodding his head as he listened.

"Not many, sir. They are contained."

Handing the large receiver back, he looked to Henry and the others and then back to his squad.

"German tanks two miles out," he stated quickly. "But we've got our own, just making it into camp now."

With a round of smiles, the corporal continued.

"Beedie. Johnston. You're needed at the front," the corporal demanded. "Straight to the front and scout the progress of those tanks. We want to knock them off before they get too close."

Both young soldiers glanced at each other worriedly, but grabbed their guns with determination, snatched some ammunition from a box, and without a word jumped over the makeshift barricade and headed as fast as they could under cover, toward the edge of town.

"Good thing, I didn't let you go, doctor." The corporal called out, making Henry turn towards him. "Things are going to get a lot nosier."

Henry dropped his soup bowl on the ground. He suddenly understood. It landed with a thud in grass, the remaining contents spilling out in a slow ooze. His hand remained frozen in front of him, unable to breathe.

"My... My wife…Eden…I must…must go to them," Henry called out to him desperately.

"Best thing you can do for them now is pray. You'd only be digging your own grave going out there right now."

Trying to remain polite, the soldier gripped his rifle showing Henry that he meant for him to stay, no matter how urgently Henry wanted to leave.

Henry stared into town, unable to think about anything but visions of tanks colliding together.

The next few hours were pure horror. A living nightmare, played out for him in the living world. Gunfire had exploded again, followed by screams of soldiers on either side, each dying for their cause. After an initial hour had passed, the first of many blasts were heard from the dreaded tanks. Each time they sounded, the civilians in the compound jumped, as the ground around them shook. The noise was deafening. With each shot, the wind whistled as the cannons fired into the air and exploded in the distance. The old lady beside Henry began to cry again, and Henry felt the need to put his arm around her and try to comfort her as best as he could. He wished that someone was there to comfort him instead.

Chapter Five

ONE AFTER ANOTHER, blasts rang out from the heart of the town. With some measure of relief, Henry deduced that the German tanks were still being held outside of the town, and the English tanks had a longer range, not allowing the Germans to return fire. With each English shot, Henry hoped that it would be the last one. It wasn't long, however, until the German tanks were finally in range, and they too began shooting toward the English in town. Each explosion brought Henry's soul closer to God. He prayed as fast as he could. On his knees he mumbled to God, to spare his family. That was all he cared about.

"God, take away everything I've worked for," Henry prayed. "Everything. I don't care. My practice. My home. Everything. Just spare Carmen and Eden. Please, I beg you. I can't live without them."

Buildings began to disintegrate. Dust flew into the air, as cannon fire missed their targets and landed on buildings, sending soot and dirt skyward. On and on the blasts continued. It seemed as if they would run out of ammo, but they never did. Henry gazed into his beloved town, seeing it disappear from his eyes. He couldn't bear to watch anymore and buried his head into the grass and sobbed.

He yawned, and blinked his eyes slowly. Amidst all of this, he was exhausted. He hadn't slept more than a few hours over the past few days, and fought to stay awake.

"Dear Lord, please make it stop," Henry continued to mumble.

His eyes flickered open and shut in an attempt to remain in the waking world as long as he could. Even with the systematic blasts of the large tanks, he eventually faded out of consciousness on the lawn within the protective barrier of the English camp. Even during sleep, his body shuddered with each explosion, but he remained asleep, dreaming all the while.

"Henry! Henry!" a familiar voice screamed from within his dream. "Get inside now!"

He remembered his parents screaming at him during the end of the First World War. He remembered the large guns that had fired their huge rounds near their home. He couldn't understand then what all the fuss was about, and why anyone would want to make so much noise. He thought that it was interesting to hear such loud noises in the sky, as the war had kept itself largely away from their farming community. He was young, and didn't understand.

"Klaus! What are you doing?" his mother's voice screamed as she clenched with a deathly grip on his arm. "I'll be there in a minute," Henry's father had screamed back, from the barn where he was securing the last of the horses. "Almost done!"

Henry drew himself into a fetal position on the dry lawn as he dreamed, remembering the whistling noise of the wayward shell that grew louder and louder, sounding as if it would land on his head. All he could remember was an impossible large explosion hitting the barn with a deafening sound. Timber and dirt flew up, and fire broke forth and incinerated the building.

"Noooo!" his mother screamed. Her grip felt so tight around his arm that his hand went purple.

Lying on the ground, drawn up like an infant and clutching his arm, Henry drifted into a less horrific state of his mind, refusing to recollect anymore of his childhood wartime memories.

As shells continued to pound the small community, Henry laid in the grass, his body refusing to wake up. Eventually, unbeknownst to Henry, the bombs lessened in severity and eventually stopped.

Day turned back into night, which brought an eerie calm, allowing Henry's sleep to go unchecked for a few more hours.

In the dead of night, Henry awoke with a jump. His heart ramped up, beating feverishly. At first. he couldn't see anything. Clouds had crept over, shading any light from the moon. A thin cloud of dust hovered silently above the ground and in the air. At first, this didn't seem out of the ordinary, as Henry was accustomed to seeing dark skies out in this small community, but all of a sudden, he realized that he didn't see ANY lights. Not from the sky or the lights of the small town. Not a flicker of candlelight, or even the dim glow from a single lightbulb. Fumbling out of his grogginess, it became obvious that there was no noise either. The first thing that hit him was that the explosions had stopped. Good news at least, there. He strained to see into town, but couldn't see what state it was in. He knew it had taken severe blows, but couldn't appraise the situation any further.

Henry swung around to question the soldiers in the camp, to find no one there. Not a soul. Not even the few civilians who had been liberated were anywhere to be seen. Henry stood up from his crouched position, and gingerly walked the few feet to the command tent and peered in. Maps and equipment still sat on tables. Gear remained stacked to the side, as if everyone had just left without touching a thing. With a quick survey, Henry noticed that there wasn't a gun to be seen. No rifles, pistols, or machine guns around. And all of the available ammo had been cleared out as well. The large radio that had been used to dispatch information to the soldiers sat on the ground, with the large handset resting to one side, almost as if whoever had used it last dropped it where they were standing, not bothering to put it back in its proper place.

With curiosity overtaking him, Henry lifted the handset, imagining hearing some chatter of news from the front lines. Gingerly placing it to his ear, disappointment set in as dead air was all he heard. Henry was utterly confused. One minute he was praying to God for all the madness to stop, and then it seemingly had. Desperation for his beloved family took over any other thoughts and he realized nothing was holding him back here. No matter how dangerous he was told that it would be for him to find his wife and child, no one could force him to stay now.

Henry hopped over the surrounding sandbags and stepped into the clearing between him and the edge of town. Slowly and cautiously he walked toward his apartment, stopping every ten steps or so to peer into the darkness imagining an enemy—or friendly, for that matter—soldier ready to pounce on him and exact some measure of punishment, none of which seemed healthy. After a few minutes Henry reached the edge of town, and it became apparent that he wouldn't be able to take the most direct route back to his home. Blocks of concrete and wood lined the alleyways and streets. The first semblances of light that he saw were the few vehicles that sat in the street, glowing from the fires that had torched them. Picking his way past the obstacle course that was once the main street, his ears finally plucked a hushed noise in the distance. He could hear faint moans and sobs coming from a building. Making his way over to one of the few remaining buildings intact, Henry paused and listened. Again, the sobs could be heard from a second-floor window. Skirting through the debris, Henry climbed the broken stairs to the room the noise came from. Through an open door, the old couple that Henry had comforted not hours before were huddled on the floor, the broken body of their son on the floor beside them. Drying blood lined the floor, as the lifeless body had multiple bullet holes in various locations. The woman, who recognized Henry immediately, looked up and through her sobs motioned to him.

"They're all dead. All of them dead."

"I'm so sorry," Henry responded empathetically.

"They're all dead. All of them." The woman continued looking back at her son, unable to control her tears.

Henry stared at them in confusion. The old man who knelt silently beside her, looked up for the first time and read the face that Henry showed.

"They have all died. All of them."

Gesturing Henry to the opposite side of the room with a glance, where a small balcony stood overlooking the opposite side of the building.

Without a word, Henry walked gingerly around the couple, who now turned their attention back to their fallen son, and stood out on the terrace and peered into the silent dark night. Several fires that still burned through the street cast a dim light. Henry surveyed the area, distressed at how the battle had littered the streets with so much debris. As his eyes focused in what little light was available to him, Henry gasped at what he saw. Horror and shock filled his face, his mouth dropping in utter amazement. He had seen his fair share of death before. In fact, it had always disturbed him how little emotion he felt at the sight of death. He dealt with it every day, and each day it seemed death felt more remote. But what he saw through the faint glow of firelight, turned his stomach, unlike anything he had felt since the beginning of his schooling and his first encounters with real death.

Bodies lay littered throughout the street. Strewn in every direction, dead soldiers held their gaze for the final time staring into eternity. Different uniforms, different ranks, all lay on the ground each forgetting each other's conflict but ending up with the same result. Henry could finally make out the outline of one of the large tanks that had rumbled into town the day before. It was burned and broken, along with everything else. Hundreds of men and machinery had met here, it seemed, in one final stand, and it looked like no one had won, or made it out alive. All of these men had fought for their team, with neither side winning.

Despite the horrific sight, Henry had to force himself away from the grim display. He had but one goal now, to find his family, and find them alive. Pushing past the elderly couple with nothing more than a sympathetic glance, he fumbled his way back down the stairs to the dimly lit street. Henry knew these streets well, and was able to skirt his way through to the edge of the community where he hoped his building still stood. With his eyes positioned on the horizon, he stumbled over loose concrete more than once. He bloodied his knee landing on a chunk of brick, which had fallen from the old church that was now half in ruins.

As he rounded the final corner, minutes later, Henry held his breath, stepping into the clearing in front of the building, shutting his eyes. He stood in place silently unable to move or breath. He couldn't open his eyes. He didn't want to find out what would be revealed when he opened them.

Finally, after a very long minute, Henry slowly let in what dim light there was, lifting his eyelids. At first, he saw what he had wanted to see, an old characteristic building, with green lawns and a cracked sidewalk that led up to the familiar front door. The way he had seen it for the first time, years ago. The image blurred and changed, however, into a sight which Henry somehow knew was going to happen. In the space where the building once stood, only rocks and rubble were piled. Henry stared for minutes, which turned into an hour. He maneuvered several times in order to enter the debris, but finally backed off realizing that there was nowhere for him to go. There was no door, no stairs, no nothing. Absolutely nothing. The apartment had taken several direct hits. Explosions had torn the very heart out of the building, and had let it bleed to death on the ground.

She could have gotten out, he thought suddenly. But looking around he knew even before hope set in, that she was somewhere in that mess, lying huddled with his daughter under tons of rock.

Tears rolled down his face, drawing lines in the soot that covered it. He looked up to the heavens screaming in his mind at God and how all of this made no sense at all. How could this have happened to him, why couldn't he have died and they lived?

"Why!" his screams turning vocal. "What possible reason could you have, to have allowed this to happen? After hours of uncertainty, wondering if his home had survived and the terror of knowing he was to spend the rest of his life alone, he looked to the horizon and screamed as loud as he could. He screamed for his wife, for his daughter, and for the God-forsaken war that had torn from him all that was dear to him. He screamed out of pain and frustration, and finally he screamed for answers. With chest heaving, and mouth quivering uncontrollably, he stopped. He wasn't satisfied with the lack of answers he was getting; as his voice grew hoarse, he knew that none of his questions would be answered. He wanted to do something, anything that would bring back his loved ones.

Only a few seconds later, light broke forth from the horizon. Minutes drew by, as Henry watched the sun enter into a new day. Red and orange beams blazed forth, catching dust and smoke, making for an awestruck sunrise. It was absolute beauty, being painted on a dirty canvas.

Henry calmed down measurably. He felt the warm rays caress his face as a father would his child. The tears continued to fall, still in anger, but more in the loss that he felt. Without anything more to do, and the way before him revealed with light, he instinctively made for his office a few blocks away. Walking slowly through the abandoned streets, he passed more than one soldier on the road, each of them with death's gripping embrace upon them. He had stopped once, looking into the eyes of the young soldier that had forced him to stay behind in the English camp. The corporal's eyes were fixd on a point in the sky, making Henry think he had been dreaming about home in his final days.

He had saved him of course, Henry realized, and knelt beside him to brush away some of the dirt from his face. "I should thank you," Henry whispered, reaching to close the Canadian's eyes for the final time. "But I don't think I can." Henry made the last few steps to his office, and in nightmarish irony there it stood, standing tall as if nothing had happened. It was almost laughable, had it not been so horrific. Buildings to the right were demolished, and buildings to the left had been gutted and burned. The old bakery stood in ruins, yet his small office still stood.

Opening the door to find everything as he had left it, with but a few books and boxes littering the floor and a measurable amount of dust on top of everything, Henry climbed into his desk chair and sat.

He didn't know what to do. He sat with the silence of death surrounding him. Picking up the familiar photo that sat on his desk, he began once again to cry. It seemed he didn't have any more tears to give; yet, he couldn't stop them if he tried. Wiping away the thick layer of dust from the picture, his mind went blank; if nothing else, he would complete his morning routine, hoping it would bring back some measure of normalcy to him, at least for a short time.

Like a zombie, Henry swept and mopped. He dusted and cleaned up his office, more than he had done for a long time. Finding an old hand-cranked record player he had kept in the back, he decided he would play some of the songs that he and Carmen had enjoyed. The music did nothing to make him feel better, but the hours went by as music and cleaning took over the small doctor's office. After scrubbing and sorting, and many records later, Henry stood in the middle of the room and realized that there was nothing left for him to do. Looking around at the spotless clinic, Henry took a deep breath and stared out of the window, hoping to see a different world outside. He wanted to go somewhere, do something, help someone. He wanted to go home and wrap his arms around his family. Sit at the table and enjoy a small bowl of soup, and read some fairy tales to his daughter, finally wrapping a blanket around her and letting her fall asleep in his arms.

Chapter Six

H E COULDN'T GO anywhere. He thought about traveling to the nearest town, about three hours away by car. But he didn't have a car. And even if he could find one that still worked, he doubted that the roads were in any shape for him to get out of the city. It would be a long walk, but that would make the most sense. But not yet, he thought. Not yet. He wasn't quite ready to leave. Without a plan, Henry sat back in his chair, wrapping his arms around his favourite picture and letting himself fall asleep.

The day waned toward night, as Henry remained motionless in his chair. After all the noise and activity of the previous days, the little town nestled in an obscure valley sat in silence. No birds could be heard chirping, no children playing in the streets, only the odd piece of brick and mortar falling to the ground. Without a plan, and his life's road at a seemingly dead end, Henry slept in his chair as if waiting for another direction to reveal itself, no matter how difficult another road would be to take. As the sun began its downward descent, light streamed in through the window striking Henry's face. The sun hung low in the western sky, casting a long shadow behind him, basking his face in an orange glow that seemed to intensify his mood. Henry squinted slightly, adjusting to the light but allowing its warmth to surround him. Sitting in his familiar chair, the doctor continued to dream of better times and scarier times ahead.

Suddenly, the light disappeared and Henry instinctively opened his eyes in surprise to see what had changed.

"Doctor...." a voice trailed, obviously in pain.

Henry jumped from his seat, seeing a young soldier standing in his doorway.

"Doctor..." the soldier repeated.

The young soldier was holding his stomach, as red liquid ran through his fingers and out onto the floor. He wavered where he stood, ready to fall to the ground.

Henry's years of experience took over, and he immediately saw a patient, neither a soldier nor an intrusion.

"What happened?" Henry inquired as he led the young man as quick as he could to the surgical bed that sat in the back of his office.

"Shot...sniper..." was the reply, growing faint.

Henry got him on the bed and moved his hands and the clothing around the wound, revealing a large hole where a bullet had ripped into his tender skin.

"Hang on, son. Hang on," the doctor encouraged.

Henry had seen this many times before. There was little hope here, he knew, but he was a doctor. An angry doctor, but still a doctor, and the distraction of the moment helped him focus on something other than his personal pain. He would do his best but it didn't look good. Grabbing a needle full of morphine, Henry stuck it into the soldier with a swift stroke, to relieve some of the pain. His next tools of choice would be a scalpel and pliers, which he would use to remove whatever shrapnel rested within the patient.

As the morphine kicked in, the young soldier's eyes drooped. His face relaxed and his head turned slightly, as he reached for the doctor's arms. And with a seemingly impossible grip, he pulled him closer.

"I'm going to die, aren't I?" the soldier asked.

"No, you aren't, "Henry lied. "Just hold on and concentrate."

"My Lizzy."

Henry continued probing for the elusive bullet fragments lodged somewhere inside the soldier's warm flesh. Sifting through tendons and bone, Henry dug deeper and deeper in search of foreign metal that would eventually take the life from this young man.

"My Lizzy," the soldier continued, as he tried to reach for his pants pocket, but couldn't quite manage it.

"Stop squirming, son. I've almost got it."

"Please doctor," he pleaded" you've got to get it to her. Please."

"You can get it to her yourself," Henry lied again, not really understanding what the soldier was asking but saying what he could to comfort him, as he extracted a large metal bullet—unfortunately to no good end, Henry realized. The boy had lost way too much blood, and the hole that had ripped through his chest had carved its way through lungs and stomach.

"I love her…. we were going to get married…" he pleaded, lying on the bed which had turned an eerie familiar red.

Henry reached to the cupboard to grab bandages and needles, still placing one hand firmly over top of the wound in an attempt to hold back the tide of blood that refused to stop. Looking into the soldier's eyes, he relaxed his reaching hand, seeing the young man's eyes flutter and his face contort. With his final breath, in between short painful coughs, the soldier looked into his doctor's eyes one last time.

Henry leaned closer to hear his patient's final request.

"Lizzy…. letter…"

And with those words, this unknown boy who had fought a soon-to-be-forgotten battle within a large war, turned his head and died.

With his heart beating no longer, the blood that had drained from the hole in his chest seeped out in a trickle, soon stopping completely. Blood littered the floor, starting from a trail that began far from his front door and out into the battlefield. Henry slowly removed his hand from this young man, his hands starting to shake and tears welling up in his eye.

After a minute of silence, Henry snapped.

"No!" he yelled at the soldier.

With unfound desperation, Henry pounded on his patient's chest.

"Breathe!" he demanded. "Breathe!" not wanting to let him go.

With every slam of his fist, blood squirted again from the hole now exposed to the air.

Slam. Slam. Down went his fist. If his patient weren't already dead, the beating he now took would have certainly done the trick.

After a dozen fruitless blows, Henry raised his arms with his fists clenched to the heavens and screamed. He screamed until he could no longer hold breath. He could no longer hold in the pain, the anguish, and all the anger that was boiling up inside of him. Sucking in another lungful of air, his body still shaking, he screamed one last time, loud and hard.

"Carmennnnn!!"

Henry buried his face in the soldier's chest, letting himself become drenched in the victim's blood and sweat. Undeterred, Henry leaned into his patient, letting the remainder of his tears and anger flow out into the empty clinic. After more than a few minutes, Henry lifted his head and let himself breathe in the cool air that drifted in from the still-open door. That was that, Henry guessed. Carmen would never be coming back. A loose tear, hanging from the precipice of his nose, dropped to the floor, pushing a small section of dirt and blood away onto the floor below.

Henry turned his attention back to the soldier. The smell of death hadn't yet set in, but Henry knew that he would have to take care of the lifeless body that lay silent on his surgical bed. Already covered in blood, and with no one to help him, Henry dragged the soldier's body out into the back, very near to where the German camp was set up only a few nights ago. A few tents still stood in place, with most of the canvas torn from their mounts. Henry could make out three bodies that lay nearby, motionless, crumpled up as if someone had thrown away a discarded toy.

"What carnage," Henry muttered to himself. No one else was around to hear him.

Henry felt that he needed to take care of his patient, this patient, with some measure of respect. It didn't seem right to have hundreds of bodies facing the open air, without the dignity of a proper burial. But for this one man, the least he could do was give him a final resting place. After sifting through some of the equipment strewn along the long narrow field, Henry finally found a small shovel, like one that would have been carried on a knapsack.

With a deep breath and sigh, Henry began to dig. Looking up into the heavens after each dozen or so shovel strokes, Henry wiped the sweat that drenched his forehead, and then continued on. This doctor was no spring chicken, Henry thought to himself, but even with most of his energy sapped right out of him, he was going to finish this task. He needed to. If his life weren't in such a shambles, he might have worried about the state his body was in. But now it felt so distantly unimportant.

After many hours, a six-foot-long, two-foot-wide, and four-foot-deep hole lay in front of the doctor. Looking around for something to wrap the body in, Henry finally ripped a piece of the torn tent canvas, and placed it around the young soldier, making sure his eyes were closed and brushing some of the blood and dirt from his face. Standing at the edge of the hole, Henry decided to say a little prayer. Maybe it was out of desperation, or obligation, but he just sensed inside of him that he needed to ask something to whom he felt was at the heart of his despair. He had yelled and screamed his anger away for the moment, leaving him tired and in more of a state of reflection. He didn't have the energy right now to get mad, and no one around him could console him. Maybe if getting mad at God didn't work, a final eulogy for this poor soul would work for the both of them. It couldn't hurt, Henry thought.

"Dear Lord." Henry began reverently. "I don't know what possessed you to allow this to happen. Why you have taken my wife and daughter, along with this terribly young man, is and always will be a mystery to me. But since you didn't let me bury my own family, I commit this boy to you, if you care to have him. I'm sure he has lived a good life, and will leave behind many loved ones, so please give them some small measure of peace, as I hope you will do for me."

With that, Henry grabbed an edge of the canvas and dragged it toward the man-made grave.

Henry paused suddenly and remembered something. Fumbling under the canvas, lifting up a coat pocket with the familiar red and white emblem sewn on top, Henry reached inside. Henry revealed an envelope that was lodged deep in the soldier's pocket. The letter, Henry thought. A single name sat on the front, *Elizabeth*. It would seem reasonable to give it to someone. It was his last request, after all.

After a short delay, Henry placed the body inside the hole, making sure the canvas covered up as much of the body as possible. He stood there looking at the outline of the body under the tarp and without realizing it, he was about to make one the most important decisions in his life so far. His gaze moved from the body to the letter, and then back to the body again. Maybe he should just bury the letter in the hole as well. That seemed a good place to leave it, considering he probably would never figure out where or who it belonged to. And what if he was killed soon enough, and the letter was lost forever, what kind of promise would that be? He hadn't the tears now to cry anymore and he was so tired that he could hardly even argue with himself. Without Carmen or Eden, what purpose did he have? What would he do? How could he live with himself, knowing he made this simple promise and then buried it along with the soldier he couldn't save?

Finally, after a long pause leaning on his shovel like a crutch, he made the decision to keep the letter. He clenched it even tighter, remembering the passion and desperation in the voice of the soldier, and how much it meant to him. Maybe he could find the same passion again, find the drive he needed to get this to whomever it was intended for. At least he could find the purpose to get clean, get fed, and wake up in the morning and start a new day. With some of the last strength he could muster, Henry poured as much dirt as was needed on top of the grave to cover it up completely.

    Henry was absolutely exhausted, dirty and hungry. By now it was getting late into the afternoon, and Henry hadn't eaten all day. He looked at his hands and clothes, and grimaced at the sight of his blood-soaked clothes that were covered in dirt and sweat. Making his way back into his office, the doctor stripped off his clothes and cleaned himself as best as he could with some towels and the little water that dripped from a small copper faucet sitting in his small sink. The water didn't look particularly clean, with a slight tinge of brown, but that was all he had for now so it would have to do. He always kept a spare set of clothes and a smock in his office and with the added benefit of a box of saltine crackers, which Henry had found out in the field, his body felt measurably better. Sitting in his office once again, Henry stared at the pool of blood and sweat that clung to the table and to the floor all around him. Looking outside at the destruction all around the office building, it didn't seem as important to clean it up this time.

    "Now what?" Henry thought to himself.

Chapter Seven

HE COULDN'T STAY here the rest of his life. And he hadn't thought about the possibility of more soldiers and armies rolling in, probably to investigate what had happened to their respective camps. There was little food, and probably not much water to be found anywhere near here. The nearest town was a good half-day's walk through the countryside. It wasn't a metropolis by any stretch of the imagination, but with some luck, the army—either army—hadn't found their way there yet. It wouldn't be that easy, he pondered. He had heard of armies laying mines throughout the countryside, especially armies that were in retreat. But he would have to risk it.

Looking outside seeing the evening drawing close, Henry thought it best to spend one last night's sleep in his beloved clinic. Looking at the grungy surgical bed, he quickly decided to take a seat at his desk, and with arms folded, rested his head and let himself fall asleep. It wasn't hard, given the events of the last few days, and as uncomfortable as it was, it was nothing compared to the tragedy his family had gone through.

After a restless night, with dreams of a better life now long gone, Henry awoke to the chill of the early morning air. With the sun still hiding its warmth below the horizon, Henry fumbled from his desk, with only the dim light to aid him. With a splash of water on his face and the last of the crackers in his belly, Henry had made up his mind. With nothing to pack, and nothing holding him back anymore, Henry grabbed the letter from his desk, shoving into his coat pocket, and walked through the open door of his clinic, not bothering to close it behind him. Stepping out into the crisp early morning air, Henry pulled his smock close to his body and tried to bundle up the best he could. He had decided on his route, but wanted to make one special stop first.

As he rounded the all-too-familiar corner, Henry paused one last time in front of the collapsed building that was once home to him and his family. Saying a silent difficult prayer Henry said a last good-bye to his former life. Looking around him, he couldn't see anyone or hear much other than some random gunfire in the far distance, or a door swinging freely banging against a bombed-out doorway. He wanted to start digging, remove every stone and boulder that stood between him and his loved ones. Looking at the immense pile of rubble in front of him, he knew deep inside himself that not only could he not complete the task alone, there was no one even to help him try. He was still so very drained, emotionally, physically and even spiritually. Placing his hand in his pocket, he felt the paper of the newly acquired envelope in his pocket, which gave him the purpose he was hoping it would give him. He would always remember Carmen and Eden, but would regret never forgetting the way in which they died, and the state he had had to leave their bodies in. Taking a deep breath, sensing the smell of death lingering in the air, Henry started out of town towards the next chapter of his life.

He decided not to turn back to look as he walked. If he were to make it emotionally, as much as physically, he would need to put all of this behind him. He always remembered being a well-centered individual, letting neither the peaks nor the valleys of life sway him too far off his emotional compass. He would need to rely on that now, he knew. Somehow, deep in his mind, he knew this journey wouldn't be easy. Somehow, he wasn't totally convinced he might be able to do it, but his family had been his life, and now that was gone. He would need another physical home, another life. Perhaps he would start up another clinic somewhere else. Perhaps he would try something completely new. He wasn't old, relatively speaking. But most of his youth, at least comparatively, had already passed him by. Of course, nothing could be done until this blasted war was over, if indeed it could ever be over. War only allowed for endings, never for beginnings. Only when it was over could he and most others start thinking of the future.

He pondered these and other eventualities as he walked through the lovely unappreciated countryside. Even though it was still spring, he was lucky the weather wasn't considerably worse. It has been known to pour relentlessly from time to time this late in the year, and nothing adds to a depressing day as much as walking through snow and mud in cow pastures without proper footwear.

When he had started out, the ground crunched as he walked. The blades of grass still tried to cling to shape with the help of the early morning frost, but gave way all too easily under the feet of the doctor. The air warmed considerably as he walked, allowing him to loosen his smock and shirt to cool off. The terrain wasn't overly rough; mostly farmer's fields with the odd fence to climb and trench to traverse. He had come here once before, he remembered, a few years ago, on a picnic with his family.

Looking out to the east, Henry remembered an old dirt road they had taken, out to an old well that stood in the middle of a field. Henry's neighbor had recommended it as a relaxing day trip, telling them that it was quite scenic and remote. It was, Henry thought, but he also remembered passing by a small cottage on the way.

"That would be such a lovely place to live someday, Henry," Carmen had said as they had passed the cottage.

"Maybe one day," Henry had responded. "We could always open a clinic out here to service the geese and mice."

Both had chuckled, thinking of nothing but the enjoyment they felt for each other's company. Shaking his head, trying to put out the memory, Henry realized it would still take hours to reach it, but it would be certainly nicer to sleep in a house than on the damp grass.

Finally, after walking for more than a few hours, and with more than a few ill-advised detours, Henry stumbled over a final fence, which led him directly to the small cottage. It sat picturesque and silent among bales of hay and a small brown and white barn.

As Henry drew closer, the first thing he noticed was the small plume of white smoke rising from the chimney. "Occupied," Henry mumbled. "Maybe a hot bun or some soup still sitting on a fire." Henry's stomach grumbled with anticipated delight. Hunger always seemed to trump circumstance. Walking up to the door, Henry gently knocked, balancing from side to side as a young teenager would, waiting for his date to open the door. Henry waited impatiently for someone to answer. Henry knocked again. The house was awfully small, so anyone inside would be sure to hear it. After a minute or so, he decided to investigate the barn. Crossing the dirt path, the doctor slid the barn door open a crack to take a peek.

"Hello…" Henry called gently, "anyone here?"

Poking his head inside, he was greeted by the sound of a cow resting on a bed of hay.

"Mmmmmooooo," the cow announced.

The doctor realized the cow was close to giving birth; with the size of her stomach it probably wouldn't be long. Returning to the food in front of her, the cow ignored Henry and left him to scan the rest of the barn. He couldn't see anything else, especially with the light fading.

"Rotten luck", Henry murmured, as he rubbed his face with his hands, showing some measure of exhaustion.

As he stood facing the barn, Henry contemplated breaking into the house, if no one showed up for a significant amount of time. He could always sleep in the barn, he figured. If nothing else a bedding of hay would be better than cold ground.

Chak-chak. The sharp sound rang out.

Henry swung around in surprise and then panic, as he turned to see the barrel of a shotgun pointing directly in his face.

"Who are you?" asked the farmer who stood, holding the weapon, steadier than Henry liked.

"My name is Henry. I'm a doctor from the town west of here," as he pointed in the vague direction he thought he had come from.

"What are you doing here?" the farmer demanded. "If you think you're going to steal something, you've got another thing coming."

Henry looked at the farmer cautiously, as the man continued to point the gun at him. He looked like a farmer should, at least in his mind. He stood close to six feet tall, with a stocky build. What hair remained on his head had turned white, telling a story of a life gone by. His face weathered and creased, he looked all too unwelcoming and angry.

"No, no." Henry stammered. "I'm just on my way to the city, and remembered your place from years ago. I was hoping to stay the night, and…and maybe get a bite to eat.

Henry tried to crack a small smile, wanting to look as innocent as he felt. He hated asking for handouts, but circumstances prevented him from debating the issue.

"On foot?" The farmer noted, "That isn't so smart these days."

"The English army destroyed my town, not days ago. I've got nothing else, no one left there anymore."

The farmer continued to stand, letting the barrel of his gun lower slightly, more because of the effort that it took, than the desire to be less threatening. Egon was a veteran of war. More accurately, he was a veteran of being a spectator of war. He was a farmer. His father was a farmer. And it gnawed at him constantly that his son hadn't taken up the same calling. He had no use for the soldiers and the machines. All he cared for was his family and his crops. Giving most of it up, to keep him in his chosen profession would be tolerated. But he didn't feel the need to tolerate those that participated in it.

"Egon," a voice pressed from behind the farmer. "Enough now, can't you see this young man's exhausted?"

Henry crooked his neck slightly to see what appeared to be the farmer's wife standing a few feet behind him. Sporting the same coloured hair and aged look, she took the few steps toward her husband and rested her hand on his shoulder.

"I don't know if I trust him, Else." The old farmer replied.

"Then trust me," Else encouraged. "It would be good to have another handsome young man around, if only for a day."

Henry smiled, feeling the loneliness she apparently felt.

After more than a few silent seconds, the barrel of the rifle dropped to the floor and the anger left the farmer's face, leaving only the weathered wrinkles that came with age and hard work. Stepping out from behind her husband, Else took her hands and rubbed them on Henry's shoulders and forearms.

"Look at you," Else empathized, "you look cold and hungry. Come in right this minute and get yourself some warm milk and some broth and sit by the fire."

Henry didn't respond, but followed the lovely lady smiling as she prodded him toward the house, leaving her husband to close the barn doors.

Henry felt warm inside as he hadn't been for a long time, sitting by the small fireplace sipping warm milk and devouring the bowl of broth that Else had promised. She worked in silence, almost enjoying pampering someone again, letting her husband sit in the corner in an old wooden chair, rocking back and forth and observing Henry's every move. Else swooped to and from the tiny kitchen, topping up Henry's cup of milk and making sure his bowl of beef broth was full. She smiled as she worked, thoroughly enjoying taking care of another person. After almost a half an hour of eating and drinking, Henry felt his hunger completely satisfied. Refusing anything more to eat or drink, he let Else take the mug and bowl, She began to clean them, finally pouring some for her husband that still sat patiently in the corner, not saying a word.

"Now tell me," Else asked, continuing to work. "About what happened to you, and your family?"

The gentleness and caring tone in her voice let all the details of the past few days spill out into the warm air. He could hold nothing back; except for the contempt he had for the German army, and the events of how the English army had saved him. He realized, of course, that he was still a German, and it would be pointless to make himself out as some sort of sympathizer to a foreign government, not knowing what that might sound like.

Henry paused many times as he described the state of his family and of how he had left them. Tears fell unabated to the ground, as Henry told them of leaving his office for the last time, deciding to head this way all on his own.

Else had stopped what she had been doing, and had placed her hand on Henry's shoulder letting her own tears fall from her eyes, and finally giving him a warm kiss on the head, as Henry finished.

"You absolutely poor thing," Else comforted.

"You didn't see our son? Klaus Redding his name is. Did you?" Egon's voice cut the silence, sounding a lot less sympathetic.

"Your son?" Henry questioned.

"He left for the army almost a year ago," Else replied, with obvious desperation in her voice, "We haven't heard or seen him since."

Henry paused for a second, not sure if his answer would be good or bad news.

"No, I didn't, I'm afraid." Henry finally decided, even though it would have been impossible to know.

Egon and Else stared at him with no expression, also unsure of whether that was good or bad news.

"What did he look like?" Henry probed.

"Oh...he was a good-looking boy," Else offered immediately. "He had such beautiful red hair and lots of freckles." After another pause, Else offered again one last time, "He was such a good boy."

Else stared at Henry in angst, hoping to hear some good news. Egon remained at his seat smoking, letting the puffs of white smoke rise in small columns to the ceiling, long past the hope of good news.

"I saw a few German soldiers, but none with that description," Henry responded empathetically. Henry wasn't sure what else to tell her. Telling her that he may or may not have seen him, but he surely saw a lot of dead young men, probably wouldn't have helped things much. All he could think to do was to put a hand on her shoulder this time, and offer her his years of a doctor's sympathetic touch.

"I'm sure he's somewhere out there. I'm sure he's just fine, and he'll come home when he can," Henry continued.

Else thought about what Henry had said, and sighed.

"Thank you, Henry."

Else moved toward her husband, taking away his bowl and with an, *I told you so* look from Egon, Else felt no better, but no worse.

Henry felt at peace in front of the fire, and with a full belly he yawned uncontrollably.

Egon stirred from the corner and while he reconciled himself to not seeing his son again, something still intrigued him from Henry's story.

"What about that letter, then?" he asked. "What does it say?"

Henry turned to look at him, and then turned toward his smock hanging in the corner.

"I'm not sure," Henry paused. "I hadn't thought to read it. I guess I figured that it was a private letter."

"How are you going to know to whom it belongs then?" Egon questioned.

"I don't know...I just assumed that I would bring it to the English army and they would take it to whomever it was addressed to."

"The English Army," Egon raised his voice moderately, "And what if this letter of yours is some sort of spy letter or something?"

"I don't really think so, Egon," Henry told him. "The boy that left it for me certainly didn't look like any spy."

"And you know what a spy looks like, then?"

"Not really, I guess." Henry looked toward the ceiling, contemplating Egon's assumptions.

"So, again, how do you know?"

"I guess I don't," Henry admitted finally "Perhaps it wouldn't be too bad to open it up and see what it says."

Henry took his time reaching for the letter, which still sat in his coat pocket. Looking again at the single inscription on the front, Henry opened the envelope carefully so as to not render it unusable. Henry gently lifted out a single piece of paper, ink crammed onto both sides, with drips of red lining the edges. With a deep breath, Henry started to read.

My Dearest Elizabeth,

I miss you dearly. I long to hear your beautiful voice, holding you as we sit on the porch, looking out at the ocean. It seems to be an eternity since I left, and I can't wait to get home. I'm writing this to you on the field of battle. We have been fighting the Germans here near Dortmund for weeks now. The fighting never seems to end, but thinking of you keeps me going. Canada seems so far away from here. Everything looks strange and different. I miss the rolling hills and tall oak trees. My love for you grows with each sleepless night. Your picture sits forever in my pocket, and looking at you brings joy to my heart. I can't wait to see you....

Henry paused, as he felt moved by the letter. Else, who had stopped her cleaning and was leaning on the counter, sighed.

"That poor boy, "Else offered sympathetically.

Henry lowered the letter to his lap, and looked at Egon.

"Doesn't sound like much of a spy letter."

"Not yet anyway." Egon replied under his breath, looking out of the window toward the barn.

Henry grinned ever so slightly, glad that his instincts were correct, helping that young man with his final request. Without being able to stop himself, he opened his mouth wide and yawned uncontrollably. Shivering ever so slightly with exhaustion Henry sat in the chair and blinked his eyes.

"Egon," Else commanded from the kitchen. "That's enough. Look how tired he is. He is going to bed right now. Go finish your chores and leave him in peace.

With a grunt Egon got out of his seat, put his pipe on the table, and made his way to the door.

"I'll go check on the cow," Egon explained as he put on his coat and headed for the barn.

"Now, for you," Else continued. "Enough of letters and get yourself to bed. There is a small bed set up for you in the room behind you."

The old mother gently took the letter Henry was holding from his lap, and carefully put it on the mantle above the fire. Looking at it briefly again, Else seemed to understand the importance of the letter. She would have hoped that her son had written something like this to her. But of course, he was alive somewhere and didn't feel the need to.

Else walked Henry to the small bedroom, wiping a tear from the corner of her eye, and opened the door for him, letting him go inside.

"This used to be my son's room." Else sighed.

"I'm sure it will be again, Else," Henry responded. "Thank you very much. I am tired, and could use a good sleep."

"Until the morning then," Else replied, as she took a deep breath.

Chapter Eight

HENRY CRACKED HIS eyelids open sometime during the early morning. He had slept peacefully for the most part, but his mind had wandered during the night and his dreams began to centre on Carmen and Eden. As had happened many times, his dreams started out wonderfully, with thoughts and scenes of old times with his family. Often pulling from real events and emotions, they would be sitting in a park or walking along a path, and enjoying each other's company. But just like his real-life events, his dreams most times took a darker turn, as his unconscious mind drew from the pain and horror in his life. It all came to a head as visions of bombs and blood with no discernible pattern drove him to awaken with a start. Breathing heavily, sweat starting to percolate on his forehead, Henry sat up in his room, blinking his eyes rapidly and letting his mind figure out what was real and what was not. After wiping his forehead and waiting until his heart's beating returned to somewhat of a normal pace, he lay back down and closed his eyes again.

"Henry! Henry!" an elderly voice called out.

Henry opened his eyes and looked out into the room.

"Are you up?" Else asked again, as Henry focused his eyes, realizing that Else had come into his room and was trying to get his attention.

"What's wrong?" Henry asked. "Have I overslept?"

"Well, no, not really. I mean you have been asleep for almost 12 hours. But I think you needed it."

"I'm sorry, I didn't realize."

"No, no...that's not what I mean," Else responded anxiously. "I mean, you're a doctor, right?"

"Yes of course; is something wrong with Egon?"

Henry could hear the trouble in Else's voice, getting out of bed as he was talking, without realizing he should have been embarrassed, having little clothes on.

"No, not with Egon," Else continued, "It's with our cow, Hilda. She's close to giving birth and we think it will happen this morning. Egon's with her, and he sounds very worried. There's something wrong we think, the baby's not coming out."

"The cow?" The doctor sounded confused. "I'm not sure what you're getting at."

"Egon's afraid we may lose her, and the baby. Could you help?" Else looked at Henry in desperation, hoping for a positive reaction.

"I'm not sure, I'm not a veterinarian," Henry responded, sensing Else's desperation. Henry paused thinking, "I did spend some time on a family farm many, many years ago, and know a little about farm births, I suppose."

Else looking still desperate, but starting to smile, replied, "I knew you might be able to help."

Henry looked into her eyes, seeing the importance of the matter, at least to her. He put his hand on her shoulder as he headed out the door towards the barn.

"I'll do whatever I can," he said reassuringly.

The doctor opened the barn door where Egon was on the ground lying beside his cow, who looked in pain and moaned heavily to prove it. It was an awful sound. While the sound wasn't quite the same as the sounds he knew from his operating table, the emotion he could sense was very similar. As with most doctors like him, Henry was able to find a way to numb to those sounds, in order to get the job done, but lately he found it hard to suppress the empathy and emotion. Egon lay on the ground with his hand slightly inside the cow. He was covered in blood, and sweat dripped from his forehead.

"What's happening?" Henry asked.

Egon turned to him, definitely without the smile Else had given in her hope.

"What are you doing here? Else sent you, didn't she?"

Henry stared back.

"I told her I could handle this."

Henry looked again at the struggling cow, and tried to envision a patient. He decided for Else's sake to treat it as one, and took a bolder stance.

"Egon. Let me get a look there. I think I can help."

"What do you know about cows and animals? This is my farm; I can handle it."

"Well your wife seemed to think otherwise, didn't she?" Henry responded frankly. "Now stand aside and let me take a look and we'll deal with this together." The doctor surprised himself in his assertiveness. He was getting into a groove, and thinking back to his youth helping on the farm, he grew more confident.

After a short pause, and another loud moan from Hilda, Egon finally removed himself from her side and let the doctor in.

"Now let me take a look at you there." Henry tried to reassure her as he would any patient. Gently rubbing her flank with one hand and feeling inside her with the other, it didn't take long for the doctor to figure things out.

"The calf is coming breech."

Egon stared back at him, giving him a slight nod.

"There's a lot of pressure there. If nothing's done, you'll lose the baby and possibly the cow."

"I agree, this is what I was thinking as well," Egon stated, taking a breath, "Sorry if I am short, she is important to us and I don't want to lose her."

"I'll need a knife, some blankets and whatever you have for a first aid kit," the doctor commanded, feeling in his element. Egon didn't say a word, but got up and briskly walked toward the house, passing by Else who had been watching from the barn door.

"Don't worry, Else," Henry called to her. "It will be painful for her, but I think things will be all right."

Henry wasn't as sure as he led them to believe, but he had dealt with this before in the human world, and figured it couldn't be different in the animal world. He wanted to save Hilda more than anything else in this world, at this particular time and this particular place. He didn't know why, but this was as important to him as it was to Egon. Looking at Hilda, he tried to envision the hundreds if not thousands of patients in his life, and stroked her neck as reassuringly as he could, given the circumstance. Of course, he wouldn't be able to talk to this patient, but in some cases that was a benefit, not a loss. His emotions may have gotten the better of him if he were able to speak, and hear a painful reply.

The hours flew by as the doctor and Egon worked on Hilda. The pregnant cow moaned and rocked as she tried in her own instinctual way to release her calf. It was a sound that Henry wasn't all that prepared for. With human patients, moaning turned to screaming and to loud words of doubt or fear. The sound of this beast seemed to echo in the barn, letting everyone know its discomfort and pain. The doctor couldn't hear anything else besides this cow. He did spot a horse, however, standing in her pen in the far side of the barn, looking on curiously, like an intern at a surgery.

Else looked on nervously for the most part, but went back and forth to the house as was needed. Finally, after what seemed all too much time, the doctor turned to Egon sewing his final stitch, and presented him with the newest addition to the barn family.

"She'll need a lot of attention for the first week or so," the doctor instructed. "Hilda's in no condition to do any mothering for the time being."

"Thank you, thank you, Doctor," Else replied, giving him a big hug, with no concern for his cleanliness. "I will take care of them. Everything will be fine."

Egon sat with his back leaned up on the stall fence, breathing heavily.

"Thank you, Henry," was all he said. Henry felt as if he didn't need to respond, but decided to leave the two animals and head to the house to clean up, feeling a lot better than he had for a long time. Somehow saving this animal felt as good as it had saving all those human patients in his years as a doctor. It was almost too hard to comprehend that just a short time ago, he was saving dozens of German soldiers, only to lose his own family. Now, only a few days later, he had saved a cow and delivered her calf. He felt the rollercoaster of emotions in his heart, and hoped that it would stop, unsure when it would.

It was some time later, when Else returned to the house to find Henry sitting by the fire warming up.

"Thanks again, Henry," Else said as she took off her boots and jacket.

Henry turned to see her, continuing to rub his hands together.

"No, thank you. It is the least I can do. I think I'm about to use up all of your hospitality soon."

"For heaven's sake, Henry."

Else looked at the young man with motherly eyes, and started to fix a hot drink on the potbelly stove.

"You are welcome here for as long as you like," Else continued. "It is nice to have such a wonderful young man as yourself around."

Henry smiled and turned back to the fire.

"I *will* stay the night, but I think it's best if I get going in the morning," Henry admitted. "If I'm going to make it to town, I'll have to start early."

He paused for a moment, rubbing his hands, letting the fire warm his face, and closing his eyes. He wanted to dive into it, if only to let that warmth surround him completely.

Letter to Elizabeth

"You're going to get us both in trouble, pumpkin", the young father laughed in his Scottish accent.

"Elizabeth!" the voice from inside the carriage called again. "It's way past your bedtime. Put down the hammer and come inside."

"Do I have to?" Lizzy asked her father, glancing over at the carriage where she and her mother had been sleeping for the last month, waiting for the house to be built.

"Pumpkin, you've helped me enough today," replied her father. "You should be doing lady stuff anyhow, and this type of stuff isn't for little lady hands like yours."

John Sr. smiled at his beautiful young daughter. It was a great time to be alive. It was the best thing he could have done, coming over here from Scotland last spring. Sailing on an old English freighter wasn't a big thrill, considering the success rate of rickety ships crossing the Atlantic, but seeing these wonderful Canadian shores certainly was making it all worthwhile.

"But father," Lizzy countered, trying to convince him, "it's not even dark yet, and I want to help, and the carriage is cramped and smells funny."

"This is your last warning, young lady," the motherly voice called from the carriage. "Your brother is already in bed, and I don't want you to wake him up."

"Go now, Lizzy" her father told her. "You can help me in the morning. And pretty soon you'll be out of that old thing and into your new house, with a room all to yourself."

"Awww." Elizabeth groaned and smiled at the same time.

Putting down her oversized hammer, the 6-year-old kicked a stone, as she walked back to her small carriage. The old wooden carriage had brought them out into the countryside, serving as a bed and a supply transporter to and from town, a slow hour away.

John turned back to his future home and stroked one of the front posts that held up the porch next to the unfinished front door. This was his home. His home, he thought gladly. Gone are the days of the smoke-filled streets of urban Scotland, worrying about finding a job, and finding enough food for his family. He was glad to never have to wonder if the rampant crime and violence was going to find its way to his house. As soon as he had found out that his wife was pregnant, he already was planning his trip to his new home. Life wouldn't be that easy here either, he knew. But he had already decided he would sell all that he owned and buy passage and a plot of land somewhere in Canada, and build a real home for his family. He could till the land, and even do some hunting and fishing for food. Soon he would finish this house and he could begin to live.

He poured his heart and soul into this house. He had started building in spring, and it was now late summer. It had been hard work. Transporting supplies back and forth from town took up a lot of time, and it had been hard on his family living out in the country with naught but a small carriage to sleep in. He slept in a tent outside the house, but he hoped to move into his brand-new building in a couple of weeks.

Back in the carriage Lizzy was bedded down tightly beside her brother, John Jr.

"Can we go for a walk down to the water, tomorrow, Mama?" Lizzy asked.

"Wader." John Jr. repeated with a yawn.

"We'll see, but for now you need to close your eyes and get some sleep," Her mother said. "There will be lots of times to go off exploring when we get settled."

Lizzy smiled as she faded to sleep, thinking of all the years she would be living here and all of the wonderful things she would do.

Chapter Nine

With a few blinks of his eyes, Henry stared up at the wooden beams that held up the roof of his bedroom. He felt better in his still fragile heart. He sighed, thinking of his family, but if he were ever to move on, he would need to remember times like these. There was still good in people, even in the worst of times. He reluctantly pushed himself out of the warm covers and put on the fresh set of clothes that hung over the seat in the corner. Else. What a wonderful lady. She had cleaned his clothes during the night for him. She even had left him a small rucksack with some spare clothing inside for him to take along.

Opening the small door to the main area, the smell of eggs and bacon washed over him like waves onto a beach.

"Good morning, Henry." Else beamed, looking from over her stove.

"Good morning," Henry replied. "Thank you for the clothes, and for the rucksack."

Egon sat in his usual chair by the door already puffing on his pipe.

"It is nothing," Else commented as she placed a fresh pair of sizzling eggs on a plate and placed it on the table. "Just some clothes our son had lying around. I'm sure he wouldn't mind."

Taking another deep breath, letting the fragrance fill his lungs, Henry stood in place. "Well, I appreciate it very much. How's the calf?"

Egon removed his pipe from his mouth with his right hand, "She's doing fine. Mother's still in some pain, but she'll heal in time."

"Come now," Else interrupted. "Sit down and eat."

"Gladly. Thank you."

Henry sat and ate, trying not to eat too fast. After his second helping, he was full and satisfied.

"I guess I shouldn't put it off any longer. The road for me isn't getting any shorter.

"We'll miss you," Else said, wiping a small tear from her eye. "And make sure you look out for our son."

"I will. And don't worry, he'll come home soon."

Henry gathered up his things, stuffing his smock in the rucksack, and with a deep breath and more than a hug or two, headed out the front door. Passing by the barn and through the gate, Henry turned to see both Else and Egon standing in the doorway watching him go.

After less than a half an hour, Henry stopped abruptly.

"Kvatsh!" Henry muttered loudly, "The letter."

Henry had forgotten it, as it still sat silently undisturbed on the mantle. Shaking his head and still arguing with himself, Henry turned to head back. That's when he noticed the small dust cloud that rose off in the distance. His eyes squinting in the morning light, Henry looked as far as he could, only able to make out a silhouette of a car bouncing on the road toward him. Henry was unsure if he should be worried or not. Of course, the sight of a vehicle in the distance shouldn't be all that troubling in normal times. But these were far from normal times. With nothing to do but go, Henry thought nothing else of it and began the walk back.

He had gotten within sight of the house, when the car that he had seen blew past him. It was obvious that the both of them were heading in the same direction and now that started to worry him. He had seen uniforms in the car, two of them. Maybe it was Else's son? Maybe it will be news about their son?

Within minutes the car pulled into the courtyard in front of the barn. Not in the best of conditions, the convertible sedan sputtered as the driver tried to turn it off. From the look of it, you would think it came straight from the front. Covered in mud and soot, and wearing more than a few dents and dings, it certainly looked out of place with its top down, sitting in front of an old farmhouse. Henry had seen this type of car before, mostly in the big cities, and usually carrying a high-ranking official of some sort. It seemed that whoever rode in it, would deem it important for the people on the street to see him being driven around, and not as much for the safety from snipers.

The two soldiers swung out, leaving the car to sputter to a stop and without knocking, opened the door and barged into the small home. Else had been sitting at the table with pen in hand, writing a letter she had decided to give to her son. Glancing over at the letter left behind by Henry, she figured now would be the time to put something on paper and maybe the fine doctor would be kind enough to take it with him as well, if he ever returned. It was difficult to write, not only because the extent of her education was limited at best, but what do you say to a son you haven't seen for so long? When you don't know where he is, and don't know if he's alive?

She had only gotten a few words down when the door crashed in. With a loud thud, the door spun around and hit the opposite wall. Two soldiers, one young and one old, stood in the doorway looking around.

"Food! Water!" demanded the older one upon seeing Else at the table.

Else looked up in horror, not sure what to do.

"Food and water, now!" repeated the same soldier.

The younger one glanced back and forth nervously with one hand by his side, resting on the holster of his sidearm. The older one, with unkempt grey hairs sticking out the sides of his head, grew more irritated.

"Do you not understand, old woman? We are hungry and thirsty. I command you to feed soldiers of your army."

Else stumbled up from her chair and clumsily gathered together some cups and looked to see what was still sitting on the stove for food.

"Of course…right away," Else stammered in fear, her heart racing.

After only a minute or so, Egon stood inside the open doorway looking in on what was going on. Hearing boot-steps from behind him, the younger soldier swirled around, raising his pistol at Egon.

"Who…who are you?" asked the soldier nervously.

"Who are you?" Egon responded defiantly, but with a tinge of confusion and fear in his voice.

"Soldiers of the army, who command you to refit us during our journey," the older soldier interjected. "Now back to it, woman."

The commanding officer turned back to Else, who had stopped to stare at what was happening in the doorway. She immediately returned to her task and set down a few mugs and poured cold tea into them.

"Don't talk to my wife that way," Egon stated firmly. "And I don't appreciate your gun pointing at my chest that way either. We are all Germans here, are we not?"

Egon looked at the young soldier's eyes, seeing the fear in them.

"Take what you came for and then be on your way."

Henry had made his way to just beyond the car in the courtyard. He had seen Egon stride out to the door and had caught a glimpse of the pistol that was pointed at him. He stood in fear, unable to think of what to do. He was no hero. What could he do? Taking fast short breaths, Henry thought that maybe there was nothing he *should* do. It sounded like they intended to be fed and outfitted and then be on their way. It certainly looked like they were in a hurry. He just stood there, out of sight, waiting for what would happen next.

"Don't take that tone with me," commanded the older soldier in a more intense voice. "We will take what we want and do what we please." Egon had never served in the army, but had taken part in his share of wars. He knew what he saw here were two men, who were scared of something and were not to be reasoned with. He bit his tongue as hard it needed, and slowly inched inside the home to where he could better protect his wife. The young soldier lowered his pistol slightly but let it follow Egon as he moved. The older one strode back and forth trying to hide his fear, trading glances from the homeowners to the doorway, which still stood open.

It was at the same time that the commanding officer and Egon both noticed the letter sitting on the mantle.

"Can...can I offer you some fresh vegetables...or some fruit...?" Egon tried to gain his attention, realizing what was going to happen.

The senior soldier ignored the offer completely, and plucked the letter from the mantle and began to read the envelope.

"What's this?" demanded the soldier, in a not so friendly voice.

Henry tried to poke his head out from behind the car to get a better look. He couldn't see anyone near the doorway anymore, and wanted to sneak a peek through the small window. He dared himself enough to lift his head part-way above the side mirror, and into the window. He could only make out the figure of Else still putting together some food and supplies for the men, but couldn't make out anything else. Even worse, he couldn't hear anything now. If it were possible, his heart beat even faster, with his legs aching to do something, to run inside or run away.

"Nothing.... just a letter someone le.... I mean just a letter for somebody." Egon stuttered trying to find some sort of logical reason for a foreign letter to be lying about his house.

"Damn English," he muttered deep in his breath.

The officer scanned the words and immediately swung to face Egon straight on.

"English!" he screamed, "What in hell is this? Some spy letter?"

The pistol that had been loosely held toward Egon returned to point at his chest as the younger soldier's eyes widened and his hand began to tremble.

"No…no," interjected Else who stopped what she had been doing and wanted to explain things better. "It's just a letter that a doctor friend of ours was to take to the army…"

"No, Else," Egon tried to stop his wife from making the situation sound more incriminating.

"Egon, it's OK. We've done nothing wrong." Else continued, turning first to her long-time husband and then to the older officer. "You need to understand, he was just passing through, and he had promised one of his patients who died…"

"Enough!" The older soldier who screamed nearly at the top of his lungs interrupted her. The veins along his temples were pulsing and he was reaching for his revolver. The younger soldier wasn't looking any calmer. His pistol hand shook noticeably and he swung his head back and forth between the three other people in the room. Sweat beads ran from his head causing him to blink.

Henry had heard the shouting from inside and had decided to enter the house. He wasn't sure what he was going to do. Maybe just convince the soldiers that he was the source of the letter and try to explain the situation. He tried to slow his breathing as best as he could, and then he suddenly realized the chances of him being taken away as a spy. He tried to put the thought out of his mind. He braced himself, gathering the courage to go inside.

"I hate this. Guns and shooting and death…" Henry muttered, "Enough is certainly enough."

"Enough!" The older soldier screamed once again, "Spies, both of you!"

"No. You're mistaken," Else tried to convince them, without any apparent success. Egon could feel something terrible was happening, and wanted to do something, but could only think of standing in front of his wife to protect her.

"What do we do with them?" stuttered the younger soldier, pistol still wavering at the chest of Egon and Else.

"I don't know. I don't know." the other replied.

"We need to hurry," the young one stated nervously. "We don't have much time before they find us."

Egon stood in front of his life-long wife, and wondered what he could do to end the situation peacefully. He wasn't known for his skills in conflict resolution and didn't have much finesse for peace talks. Seconds of silence cut through the air like a knife through a piece of hardwood.

"We have to go...sir," offered the young one, stuttering. "And they might tell them where we are."

"I know," the other replied, irritated. "I know."

Egon didn't like the sound of that. He looked down to where he saw a large cutting knife sitting on the table in front of him. Not much use against two guns, but certainly better than nothing. And if he was forced to.... he thought.

Henry had had enough all right. The silence was worse than the yelling. He had to go in. Lifting his cramped body from his crouching position, he rose to enter, but before he could take one step...

Bang!

Henry instinctively dove back behind the car in horror.

Bang! Bang!

Two more shots rang out from inside the house. Henry dove back behind the bush a few yards beside the car. It probably saved his life. Seconds later, the two soldiers ran out of the house with pistols in hand. The older one came first, blood noticeably sprinkled on his uniform, the younger one second, holding a loaf of bread in his spare hand. Without looking around, the older one jumped into the driver seat of the convertible, and forced it to start. Without waiting to see if the other soldier had made it in or not, he hammered the gas pedal and left a spray of gravel and dirt behind him as he drove off. The younger soldier barely made it into the back seat as he drove off.

Henry shook all over. He couldn't move. Silence washed over his ears, as nothing audible stirred from the house. Henry couldn't hear anything but the pounding of his heart, and even the sounds of a bird chirping in the air escaped him. Pessimism crept into his mind. He knew that something horrible waited for him inside. He wanted to remain positive, but maybe the days of being an optimist were behind him. Too much bloodshed with only little glimpses of joy had invaded his soul the past week. He remained in place for a few minutes longer, holding on to hope that Egon would call for him, or even better, would walk out with his wife.

After realizing that wasn't going to happen, he almost forgot his oath that he had sworn so long ago. Yes, to do no harm, but also to save life as best he could. He was a doctor after all, wasn't, he? If there was something he could do, shouldn't he get himself in there and do it? He almost forgot that. Standing outside wasn't putting his practice into use. Looking over his shoulder with every step, even though he saw the two German soldiers leave, he entered the house.

Lying on the ground was Egon. Two bullet holes, clearly outlined in red, opened onto his chest. Beside him not one foot away was Else, one terribly evil bullet hole laughing at him from the dead centre of her face. Blood was pooling from behind them, and Henry, without much hope, reached to check Egon's pulse, but felt nothing. A large lump gathered in his throat as tears poured from his eyes. He wanted to cry out, but didn't. He just stood over the bodies in silence. Even with this pitiful scene in front of him, he doubted that he would ever be able to shed any more tears. "The well's all dried up," whimpered Henry as he raised his eyes to the heavens. "And so is my faith in you."

It took him the rest of the day to pull the two bodies out of the house and bring them out to the garden. He had found a shovel in the barn and started digging. Without talking, praying or crying,

Henry dug two graves side by side and gently placed the bodies inside. He had thought to put them together, but decided that what sounded romantic probably wasn't very kind. Even though no one would most likely ever disturb them, he knew that eventually the decomposing bodies would mingle together and eventually collapse on each other. And that didn't sound very romantic. After finally covering the graves with dirt and stones, he thought about making some sort of gravestone or cross. In the end he just took the long handled shovel and broke it in half, removed the spade, and stuck each half in front of a grave. Tired and hungry, he returned to the house, deciding it would be stupid to head back where he was going tonight after what had happened.

He sat on the chair in the main room and stared at the pool of blood that was on the floor. His mind desired to clean it, but his heart didn't let him. He just sat there, for more than an hour, thinking of his family, and then about Egon and Else's son, whom he hoped was already dead.

As his stomach turned, he leaned toward the stove which still smoldered ever so slightly and lifted the lid to a pot that sat on top. At least one helping of stew still sat inside. It was cold, but that could be remedied. Grabbing some wood from the side, he placed it in the stove and fanned the tiny embers back into life. Letting the stew come back to heat, he thought that a meal would taste slightly better with a clean pair of clothes and a wash.

Feeling not as guilty as he should have, Henry grabbed an extra pair of clothes from their son's bedroom and washed up as best he could with what lukewarm water he could find. Finally, he sat down to a bowl of stew and some leftover bread the murdering soldiers didn't grab. Taking a deep breath and feeling a chill in the air, Henry opened up the stove again, placing a pile of logs inside, and hobbled to the bed. His eyes closed before he hit the pillow and was gone to the world.

Chapter Ten

NOT A DREAM broke his sleep, drifting in a world with no light and no depth, his mind on cruise control unable to contemplate the events that plagued him. That is, until he dreamed of a warm crackling fire. Somehow it didn't feel welcoming. In fact, it felt warm. It FELT warm. His eyes opened in an instant to see smoke rising from the main room and drifting unimpeded into his room. He shot out of his bed to see the bulk of the main room in flames.

"Agghh! The stove!" Henry cried.

Realizing that he had forgotten to close the lid, he scanned the room to see if there was anything he could do. It was immediately apparent that this fire would stop for no one. He grabbed his rucksack that sat on the floor as he dashed for the open air. Something tugged at him to stop. With fire crackling around and above him, and embers falling from the ceiling as raindrops, Henry rubbed his eyes in the dense smoke and saw his traveling companion. There, sitting on the floor staring him in the face, was the letter. Staring at him with unseen eyes, demanding for him to pick it up and continue carrying it to its final destination. Henry didn't have time to argue with himself, but brushed away the few embers that already were trying to claim the letter as fuel, and rushed out of the house into the night.

Henry stood a hundred feet away watching the house sink to the ground. Egon's home and hopes would be no longer. The ceiling collapsed first, dropping down inside the four walls that had held it up. A burst of flames poured out of holes that opened in the roof as it fell. The simple wooden structure didn't stand a chance. Smoke filled the sky, rising up in the early dawn as the night drew a pale blue mantle. Glass shattered as the walls buckled under the lack of support and swayed, falling to the ground. Henry glanced at the barn wondering if it would go next. Luckily there was no wind, and fire and smoke rose straight up into the sky, new smoke compounding against old smoke until completely opaque.

Henry couldn't help but stare at the tragic scene. He felt the same thing as he did when looking at the remnants of the buildings in his little town, but somehow this didn't have the same sting in it as that had. Of course, he was mad at himself for letting this happen. Of course, he hated those two soldiers for killing his new friends and surrogate parents. But he had realized that destruction seemed to follow him, and this event was apparently a continuation of that path. Henry scanned the horizon to see if anyone else could see what was happening. It was still dark enough that the smoke would be hard to see, and the flames had shot up and back down fast enough anyone not directly watching probably would have missed it. It seemed a moot point anyway. No one lived for miles around and Henry couldn't see any movement in any direction. No firefighters would be coming to rescue this house, even if they could.

After watching wood and metal sink to the ground, turning into a large smoldering pile, Henry faced the road ahead. Taking another deep sigh, he decided that there was nothing for it, and would make the journey to the next town. He figured at a good march he could arrive sometime late into the evening, but had plans to find shelter along the way. Somehow, he didn't have the energy to hurry. Yes, the letter would find a home there, but he certainly felt that it could wait an extra day if that's what he decided to do.

Before he started out, he felt the need to step inside the barn and check up on the cow and calf that he had helped days before. "I hope you make out okay," Henry whispered gently to the cow. "Take care of the little one.". Amazingly, Hilda was already standing in her pen and was feeding on what was left of the straw inside it. She seemed in some discomfort still, as she shuffled around the tiny pen, but Henry figured she would make it. In fact, her situation seemed a lot better than his right now. She had a home and a newborn with nothing to worry about except where to find her next meal. Henry realized that even her situation would change though. With no one to look after her to make sure she was milked and fed, her plight might not be as envious as he thought. But for the time being it felt good to think that she would be fine. Looking to the back of the pen, Henry gazed upon Hilda's new calf. Impressively, she too was already standing and pushing her wet nose against the straw, still curious over each new thing she encountered. He took the time to stroke the neck of the tiny calf, feeling the warmth inside her, longing for a new birth for himself. The calf looked into her doctor's eyes cautiously for a moment, but soon rubbed her nose against his pants, almost as if sensing the desperation and quiver in Henry. He thought briefly of taking them with him on his journey to the next town, but decided it would be too hard on Hilda, not to mention the calf. In a final gift to his patients, Henry grabbed a pitch fork that stood to the side, and heaved in a large pile of hay into the pen for future consumption. The best he could do for them now, was give them extra food, and let the small fragile calf suck on her mother's milk as much for comfort as for nourishment. Better for her to recover here, Henry thought, in familiar surroundings even with her future uncertain. His thoughts quickly strayed to his own circumstance and longed to see his daughter, and hoped that somewhere in heaven she was happy and playing harm free with her mother. He desperately wanted to be with them, but tried just as quickly to put it out of his mind. If not for this confounded letter he held in his hand, his motivation to keep moving would surely be lost.

    After delaying himself here for a while, he stepped out onto the road and began the journey he hoped would end in a better completion. He grabbed his rucksack, stuffing the letter inside his jacket and marched ahead. He couldn't help but take one more look back as he walked down the road, seeing the skinny trail of smoke still rising into the air. He shook his head slowly, realizing that in some way he envied Egon and Else. It would have been a lot less painful for him to remain inside the house as it burned. His future was so unclear, like fog that clung around him on a dreary day. If not for his immediate mission, there would be literally nothing for him to do.

As the morning sun broke through the horizon, he felt somewhat better, if not less chilly. It felt like it would be a warmer day and outwardly hoped that spring would finally take back its grip from winter's grasp.

The morning came and went without mishap, and Henry made decent time. He encountered no one, and saw little life. The odd bird and rodent stopped to say hello, but were unable to take away from the loneliness of the journey.

Henry had stopped briefly for lunch, and sat down on an old fence post that had fallen down and made for a slanted seat. He munched on the few scraps that he had left in his rucksack, while he sat letting the sun warm his face. He ate in silence, a few crumbs falling from his mouth onto the ground beside him. Looking out onto the fields, he tried hard to not think of anything at all. Like an ocean, the fields stretched out, intersected every once in a while by a post or a new type of crop. One single tear formed in his left eye. It grew as he sat, eventually letting go and slowly trickling down his cheek, curving around his nose and pausing on the top of his lip. Within a moment, it fell in a drop onto his chest, leaving a tiny mark on his coat. Henry had allowed it to fall without wiping it, hoping not to acknowledge it. His heart was still aching, but he wouldn't let his mind take the bait anymore; dwelling on the past and his uncertain future felt useless and pointless.

When he had finished his small lunch, Henry continued to walk. He was uncertain of the route he was taking, but after all, there was only the one road and he figured that despite possible dangers it would be safer to stay on the road for the time being. It was some time before Henry came across a similar intersecting road. Much like the road he was on, this road stretched for as far as he could see. More gratifying was the fact that a signpost was erected to the left of the intersection. It read that his destination was still 15km away. Looking up into the sky, Henry felt tired. The sun had followed its arc across the sky until it now sat slightly above the horizon. Walking another twenty minutes, his legs began to feel heavy. He shouldn't have been all that tired as he had stopped more than a few times to rest, though that was probably the reason he hadn't reached the town by now. What he had reached, though, was a small grove of trees that stood along both sides of the road. It stretched for at least the next few acres, he figured, and thought that maybe now was the time to find a place to rest for the night. He could probably make it to town before it got too dark, but figured it might be for the best if he started early in the morning and got there with some light to guide him.

Henry was cautious, and wandered slightly into the trees to find a more secluded spot to bed down. After wandering around for a bit, he was pleasantly surprised to find some wild berries growing between a few trees. They were still unripe, but even with the tart taste; it felt good to eat a few. It took some time, but the doctor settled on a soft spot between the roots of a magnificent oak tree. It stood tall and mighty with large branches filled with green leaves.

Henry wasn't much of a camper. He had, in his early years, spent the night in the wild once or twice, but usually with some sort of tent or covering. He certainly wouldn't have been caught in the open without proper gear, though. Sleeping in the open with only a few clothes to warm him didn't scare him really—not as much as the anticipated chill did.

He was amazed, though, with how warm a bed of leaves could be if you buried yourself inside them. Henry snuggled himself among the variously shaped leaves and heard them crunch, as he burrowed out a sleeping hole for himself. Wiping away the few damp leaves that stuck to his face, Henry lay down, as the last of the light faded away, and stared up at the nighttime sky. His tummy was rumbling and grumbling, but he refused to acknowledge it. It was like his stomach was calling out to him in panic, wondering what was happening. The stars shone with amazing brilliance. Like pinpricks in a large black canvas, they stared at him with eternal eyes. Offering no hope or return to better times, Henry didn't find them as attractive as he should have. In better times he would have really enjoyed it, but instead he just stared out into the air, letting his eyes droop until he fell asleep. Henry slept that night in some measure of peace, and for the first time, without realizing it, forgetting to think about his family. At one point during the night he thought he heard the sound of gunshots and screaming in the distance, but they were muffled and a long way off. He just rolled over and ignored his imagination.

Henry awoke matter-of-factly, and brushed off the leaves that clung to him with the help of the early morning dew. The sun was cresting the horizon and Henry anticipated the warmth he hoped it would bring. He decided to eat a few more of the berries he had found the day before, but after a handful he had had enough of the bitter taste. With nothing more to do he found his way onto the road and continued onward.

After a half an hour or so the road he was on began to bend, with the trees still lined up on either side. He had little time to notice the vehicle that came zooming toward him. Muffled by the trees, and obscured by the curve in the road, the car came upon Henry quickly. Henry stopped in his tracks in fear. The vivid memories of his last encounter with a vehicle washed over him. He wanted to jump to the side of the road and hide among the trees, but there was little time. The vehicle, however, was quite different to the last one. More of a family sedan, it came rushing toward Henry. Standing in place, the doctor watched as the driver finally noticed him on the road and braked heavily to come alongside of him.

"It's over!" one of the passengers yelled out.

Henry stared ahead, without expression. The car contained a full load of German men, seemingly all farmers. All in their late thirties or early forties, they gleefully hollered and yelled among themselves and at Henry.

"It's over, man! Haven't you heard?" the driver screamed out as he propped himself out of his window to stare at Henry over the roof of the car.

Henry continued to stare, and then finally added, "Heard what?"

"The war. It's over!"

"Really?" Henry asked, not able to properly comprehend the news. "When?"

"It came over the radio this morning. Can you believe it?" another one of the men answered joyfully.

"Wow," was all Henry could muster.

Before he could think of anything else to say, the driver popped back into his seat, and rammed the car in gear.

"What day is it today?" Henry called out as the car inched forward.

"May 7th!" yelled the passenger in the front seat, "Remember it, my friend, the day your life started over."

The driver hammered the gas, and the old sedan pitched forward with a chirp and sped along the road.

Henry wasn't sure why he had asked what day it was, but remembered he had lost track of the days and figured he needed to know. Somehow important events are always associated with the date they took place on. As a child he was told the dates when the First World War had started and ended, and this certainly seemed as if it would be an important event. He remained standing in the street for around ten minutes, his mind continuing to try to grasp the news he had just heard.

It was great news to be sure, but somehow, he couldn't figure what meaning it had for him. He then remembered his family again.

He had forgotten about them for a while and that made him sad. But without them, the war ending didn't have as much meaning. It seemed silly to think that he wanted the war to continue, but it was during the war that he still had had a family. During the war he still had a home to go to. During the war he had warm arms to hold him, and that was what he missed the most. In a sense he hoped the war wasn't over, because that would be just another reason for him to accept that another stage in his life was beginning. Again, he felt like crying, but his anger at his own situation wouldn't let him.

Henry took a deep breath and began to walk again. Not feeling in any particular rush, he continued slowly toward town, trying to empty his mind of everything.

Chapter Eleven

THE ORANGE AND red fire crackled, as it burned in the large fireplace that sat in the den. It was the first thing that had been built in the house. Various sizes of grey rocks lined the edges of it, with a large cedar mantle overhanging it. Lizzy sat in her favorite chair that her father had built for himself, when he had been a young man. A grand old rocking chair with a high back, that creaked ever so slightly when it rocked. The wood was old and worn now, and the varnish rubbed down almost to the bare wood on the bottom, and the seat felt like it had sunk slightly from the years of use. It offered her some measure of comfort these days.

Elizabeth sighed, and put down the scarf that she was knitting. She looked out from the room, through the window and into the yard that stood in front of the house. It was still covered in white. Even with the seasons changing, the winter refused to give up its power to spring, and had decided to dump another few centimetres overnight just to prove the fact. Beyond the fence posts at the edge of her yard, she could still make out the beginning of the ocean waves that lapped against the shore, below the small cliff on which her house stood.

This was a beautiful country. God's country. Her father had come here from Scotland when he was a young man, and had built this house almost thirty years ago. There was little here when he had built it, and little had changed. He and her mother had died from some form of influenza years ago, and had left her and her brother to take care of it ever since. John Jr. and she had taken care of the old house, patching the roof when it needed it, painting the doors and window trims, neither one of them having any desire to ever leave this place. That is, until the day she had met Alan. After nearly a year of courtship she was ready to leave this wonderful place and start her own life in a home that she and Alan would build. It would be close by of course. She would never leave Nova Scotia, and they would live happily ever after. Lizzy smiled. Despite the present circumstance, she still smiled. The war had put all of their plans on hold. Both John and Alan had gone. It had been four months already. From Alan's last letter, at least they were being stationed together and hadn't really seen much action yet. From the tone of his words, he was even predicting an end to it soon.

Soon, they would come home, and everything could get back to normal.

The town became visible within an hour. At first a few small houses with large barns lined the outskirts. Seeing them there gave him a chill, remembering the destruction of Egon and Else's home. The odd farmer could be seen, plowing the large fields on either side of the road. Henry thought it curious that they would be out in their fields, if the war had ended. Yet, give it to the German farmers to do their chores even if the world, as they knew it, had changed again. Mother Nature wouldn't wait for them, he thought, and in a sense that made Henry feel better.

As more roads intersected his own, which eventually became a street, he entered the town unsure of what to do next.

At first, he didn't notice anything out of the ordinary, but as he continued on, he realized that there was a lot of activity going on. The town was a lot larger than his; not a city of course, but the odd building rose much further into the sky than those in his did—or they had. They were all rubble now, along with the many bodies inside. As he walked, with no particular direction in mind, more and more vehicles skirted to and fro, most of them clearly army vehicles—English ones, at that. The odd civilian car drove past, but what caught his attention the most were the vehicles that bore a familiar red cross on the side. It seemed there were many more than usual, and he decided to follow them, if he could, to their destination. Henry continued on along the sidewalk of the street where he saw two army ambulances drive by, and hurried his step, somehow out of instinct. The sound of those that needed care still tugged at him. It was what he was born to do, he had always thought.

As he marched, he came across an old schoolhouse that sat on the corner. It looked in disrepair and it certainly didn't look as if it was being used much as a schoolhouse these days. A half-dozen army vehicles stood at the ready in front, and army personnel marched in and out. Henry stopped for a moment and watched as the various ranking English soldiers would hop out of their vehicles and stride in or out of the building, saluting whomever they encountered. It was amusing to see them salute each other so frequently. He did find it odd that there would be so much activity there. He didn't care for the politics of war much, so he hadn't thought to consider this some sort of base. As he stood in place watching, one of the soldiers strode over to him, standing much too close for his comfort.

"Can I help you, sir?" asked the soldier.

He was a large middle-aged man, probably with some rank, although Henry didn't know how to read his foreign medals and honors. His eyes certainly gave him the aura of authority. Henry sensed he was being scanned, and suddenly felt very uncomfortable.

"You are German, aren't you?" asked the soldier, not allowing much time for Henry to answer.

"I...I am", quivered Henry.

"What are you doing here, then? Can I help you?"

Henry thought his voice didn't sound very helpful, and he should probably say something to give reason for standing there.

Henry noticed the soldier giving him the once over, probably scanning for weapons of some sort. All of a sudden, he remembered the letter he carried.

"I...I'm looking for a place...I mean for a person to give this letter to." Henry tried as best as he could to sound deliberate, but the intimidation of the soldier made him stumble. He started to pull out the letter, which was sitting in his rucksack.

"Ease up there, pal," remarked the soldier as he placed his right hand on his pistol, which sat on his belt.

"No, no. It's just a letter, here." Henry slowed himself down and slowly pulled out the letter as if taking out a live bomb. He gently lifted it to show the soldier.

"What's this?" he asked, taking the letter in his left hand, without removing his other hand from his pistol.

"It's a letter I was given about a week ago, from one of your men." Henry tried to explain. "He was in my office and died, but asked if I could deliver this for him before he passed away."

"Died?" the officer questioned, looking quickly at the single name written on the front, lowering the letter to look Henry square in the eyes. "What soldier?"

Henry realized that he was painting himself in a corner. He was no Nazi supporter or anything, but his answers weren't exactly helping out the situation.

"I'm a doctor." Henry started to explain. "I live.... I mean I lived a few miles from here. The town was destroyed in the war, and I was trying to save as many as I could, but I couldn't save this one." Henry was talking faster than he should have, and took a look at the soldier who continued to stare at him without blinking an eye. "He gave me this letter to his fiancée, on the operating table before he died. I guess I felt obligated to bring it to someone."

The soldier didn't make a move but turned his eyes down to the letter in his hand; then he took his other hand from the gun and opened the envelope up to read it.

"Maybe I can leave it with you, then?" Henry asked. All of sudden he became conscious of the fact that this could be the last he would see of it, and finally would have nothing more to do with it.

As the soldier scanned the letter, another loud voice broke through from behind him.

"Captain Arnold," another soldier cried, as he ran up to him from inside the schoolhouse.

The higher-ranking soldier lowered the letter slightly and turned to face the voice.

"Captain," the younger soldier spoke again, as he panted from running.

"Yes, Corporal?" responded the captain, taking his eyes off the letter and Henry.

"We have another group pinned down twenty miles to the east. They request air support."

"Thank you, Corporal, resume your duties"

"Yes sir," the corporal saluted the captain, and jogged back inside the schoolhouse.

Henry stood in place, not daring to move or say anything. The captain took another quick scan of the letter and handed it back to Henry.

"Doctor, eh?" he asked rhetorically, looking back into Henry's eyes.

"Yes." Henry answered anyway.

The captain took a brief look toward the schoolhouse and returned his gaze toward the doctor.

"You'll need to take this to our temporary dispatch office. It's located in a local theater a few blocks away."

"Thank you." Henry gently took the letter from the hands of the army man and remained standing in place.

The captain turned to leave.

"By the way, we're getting a lot of wounded here. We've set up a large regional infirmary in the local hospital and are getting patients from miles around. Any help you can give would be appreciated."

Henry stood in place without saying a word, but continued to watch the captain stride away with some purpose, back to his temporary base. He sighed, both in relief he wasn't arrested and knowing his journey wasn't going to end just yet, then tucked the letter inside his coat pocket and continued on. The street traffic rumbled to and fro as he walked, and in a way he was relieved to know that there was still life in the world. It was strange to see so many English soldiers around. He certainly wasn't a linguist or anything, but he could tell there were many Americans, Canadians and British soldiers about. Without making a firm decision in his mind, his legs carried him toward the local hospital. He desperately wanted to get rid of this letter, but it could wait a few more hours, and he was a doctor after all, and sick people came first.

As Henry rounded the next corner, the first thing that was apparent was that the local hospital was ill-equipped and too small for the amount of patients that were entering. Stretchers were carried out of the back of military ambulances, civilian ambulances and even the odd car. With military procedure, injured were directed immediately to various locations, with the most desperate heading instantly into the building and those that could wait longer for care, under large tents set up in the parking lot.

The disturbing thing was the long lineup of patients and transporters that had to wait to be evaluated before they could move to their location. As Henry walked a lot closer, he could also see that some of the patients lying under the tents were getting little or no attention, and some of them certainly could use a change in location. Henry jogged the last few steps to the entrance of the hospital and sought out the person he thought looked like the physician in charge.

"Can I help?" Henry asked

Without turning his head to see who was asking, presumably recognizing the German accent, the large doctor replied, "You a doctor?"

His accent was thick, and Henry recognized it immediately as British. The tone certainly sounded as if it was half-joking.

"I am." Henry responded directly.

The British doctor gestured for the young army soldiers who were carrying a patient in front of him to stop, and turned to face Henry.

"Really?" he questioned, "Army?"

Henry realized quickly that there might be something fishy about his volunteering if he were from the army, considering the Germans had just surrendered.

"No. Civilian," Henry responded.

"Can you handle triage?"

"Yes."

"Start under the tent and fix what you can." The large man looked past Henry and spotted a nurse shuffling in and around the cots underneath the green tent. "Emma!"

The British doctor paused quickly to look back at Henry. "Your name?"

"Henry."

"Work with Henry here, he's going to give you a hand over there!" the Brit called again.

"And if I can't fix them?" Henry asked as the other doctor turned his attention back to the patient lying in front of him still on the stretcher.

Without turning, he quickly responded, "If you're sure they can be saved, send them in; if they're a lost cause, move on to the next one."

It could have sounded callous but Henry knew what he meant, and turned to the tent. Putting down his rucksack on an empty chair and removing his smock from inside it, he put it on and quickly moved under the tent and got to what he did best.

Chapter Twelve

THE NEXT FEW hours were good hours for Henry. He was in his element now, and decisions were made swiftly and accurately. Patients were being sewn up or passed along to whatever location they needed to get to. His heart did ping ever so slightly when he made the decision to disregard a patient, if they had deteriorated to the point where they couldn't be saved, but luckily there weren't many, and even more luckily, he didn't have the time to dwell on it. His life and family took another back seat to what was at hand, and strangely enough when his mind did center back on his personal situation, it was the letter he carried in his pocket that he thought about. He didn't really think anything specific about it, just that he felt the need to get rid of it. Looking into the eyes of so many injured soldiers, the final gaze of the young soldier that died in his office still burned in his mind.

The civilian doctor moved from bed to bed with ease, having little difficulty with the task at hand. Moving from patient to patient, he thought it strange how soldiers reacted differently to their particular situation. Death, or at least the fear of death, manifested itself in different forms with each patient. Some called out to their mothers, some to their wives or children. Others would swear as loud as they could or blame the army for their predicament. Working on one particular patient made Henry feel somewhat eerie, to be honest. Surveying the soldier's injuries, he noticed the patient didn't do anything or say anything, just remained lying on the bed with not one but two bullets and their fragments embedded in his chest. He merely lay there, almost without pain and took his injury in stride. If it hadn't been for an instinctive flinch on his touch of the wound, Henry would have thought him completely sedated already. More than a few, though, called out to God and Heaven to deliver them from their pain, or at least to end it. Henry heard the calls, but inside doubted that they were being reached. They would hold up their arms and beg for forgiveness, or even bury their face in their hands cowering in shame. Henry did remember when he had called out to God. There had been times when even he felt the need to ask God for a special favour. Thinking back, he remembered just such a call to the heavens, hoping to find a way to meet his love, Carmen. He remembered going to church with his family every Sunday as a child, but as he had gotten older those trips had gotten farther and farther apart. And with what had happened to him lately, and his seemingly growing anger at God, he quickly dismissed the idea that any God, who supposedly cherished life, would be listening.

"Doctor?" the nurse interrupted his brief mental wandering.

Henry turned to her.

"We've got a bleeder over here." She pointed to the young soldier who occupied the bed where she was standing and gathered up tools as Henry drew closer.

In that instant, Henry thought of his dear wife Carmen, but quickly closed his eyes, then opened them, washing away the memory and continuing his work.

By the end of the day, and as evening drew close, the steady stream of wounded had diminished to a trickle. The last of the stitches were placed and the nurse continued to wipe away blood and sweat from the remaining patients that lay under the army tent. The German doctor leaned against a tent post and wiped away his own sweat from his forehead and took a long deep breath.

"Tired?" a voice boomed from behind him.

Henry recognized the strong British accent as the doctor he had met early in the day. He turned to meet the voice.

"A little," Henry admitted, looking more exhausted than he wished to admit.

"Great work out there, doctor," the Brit complemented. "It's a testament to your skill that we didn't get too many patients from you inside."

"I had a great helper," the German doctor replied, in his very best English. "But we did have to send some to the morgue."

"Not many, from what I heard. Good job."

"Thank you. Are we all done here?"

"I think we can wrap the rest up, there will be a few more to come, but I think we can handle it from here."

Henry groaned, as he removed his bloody smock and used a cleaner section to wipe away more sweat from his face and hands.

"Where are you staying?" asked the army doctor.

Henry paused, remembering suddenly he didn't have a place to spend the night. He didn't realize that he would be tied up for so long here.

"I'm not sure," he admitted. "I'm actually here to deliver a letter for someone, and hadn't thought about it."

"A letter, eh? Well there is a distribution centre in an old theater I think, but as for room and board, I'm sure we can help you out for a night or two."

"That would be nice, thank you," Henry replied immediately, anticipating a good night's sleep.

"Tell you what," the Brit added. "Go deliver your letter, and I'll make room for you in the hotel across the street. There should be a hot shower and a bed for you."

The army doctor took another look at the German, and smiled at his appearance.

"And someone to wash those clothes for you, too."

Henry smiled back, hardly remembering the last time he did.

After dumping his rucksack with the attendant at the hotel, he made his way down the street to the old theater, hoping to be finally rid of his letter. As he walked, he pictured the young soldier lying on his table, back at home, and wondered what he had been thinking in his final moments. He wondered if the man's thoughts were similar to what he was thinking as he looked upon the remnants of his apartment building. Did he regret not seeing Elizabeth one last time, or was it more that he feared what she would be like, knowing her brother was already dead as well. Henry hurt inside, having no one to really mourn his losses with. He had no real family anymore, his parents and siblings having passed away years ago. He did have a few uncles and aunts, but hadn't talked to them in a long time, and had separated himself, intentionally or not, from anyone else he was related to. He didn't even have any friends to speak of. His work and his family had been his life, and both had been ripped from him.

"Curse you, God," he whispered, with his teeth clenched.

He hoped that Elizabeth would take comfort in this young man's last words and hoped she would have someone special to console her.

Without having to ask for any directions, Henry made his way to the old theater that seemed to have a lot less activity than the hospital did. His heart sped up with the anticipation of delivering the letter. Until this moment, he didn't appreciate how much the letter had become part of his short new life. He felt close to it and to what it had inside, even though he hadn't even read it all. His life had changed so drastically since the war found his home, and this letter gave him some purpose, and now he would have to deal with getting on with his life. Fulfilling the young soldier's last wish was becoming strangely such an important burden; not only to bring some completion for the soldier's loved ones, but to give Henry some of that same peace in a surrogate sort of way.

He wandered in without being noticed and found a lone soldier sitting in a chair behind a makeshift desk consisting of bricks and plywood.

"Can I help you?" the soldier asked as he rose from his chair.

"I have a letter from an English soldier that needs delivering," Henry said in his slight German accent, as he started to pull out the letter from inside his jacket.

Henry could see the soldier's eyes grow worried with fear, as his hand dropped to his sidearm. It was not like he wasn't used to this by now, but he hadn't stopped to realize what it would look like to see a German man, with bloodstains on his clothing walk into an army-controlled facility, even one as empty as this one.

"A letter..." the army man asked, more interested in the German standing in front of him, than in what he wanted.

"I was sent here by one of the Captains.... Captain Arnold. To deliver a letter from one of your soldiers," responded Henry, quickly remembering the captain's name, hoping that would instill some confidence in the soldier.

"Captain Arnold sent you?"

Obviously, the name had the desired effect, calming the soldier's nerves considerably.

"Yes, can I leave it with you?" Henry asked, producing the letter and holding it up in front of the officer.

The man in charge took another look at Henry and then a glance at the letter, removing his hand from his sidearm, but remained standing. He smirked and shook his head slightly looking at the single word on its front. It was clear that he was still more interested in Henry than he was about the letter.

"You can leave it inside; there is a pile of mail waiting for sorting." The soldier pointed to a door behind him that led to the main auditorium, which sat open. "Someone will get to it, in time."

"Thank you." Henry offered, slowly moving past the man, who still kept his eyes on the doctor, making sure he didn't show signs of carrying a weapon.

As he slipped past the doors and into the dimly lit room, he wasn't ready for what he saw. Sitting on rows of seats were plywood sheets acting as tables for the immense amount of papers that sat on them. Stacks and stacks of correspondence rested on old lumber, with no form of sorting apparent. Henry didn't even know where to put the letter. He just stared at the piles of envelopes and parcels wondering where they were all going, and when they were going to get there.

Taking one step back, Henry called to the attending officer, "Where should I put it?"

"Anywhere," the voice called back through the doors. "Just throw it on the pile."

Henry looked down at the name written on the envelope, "Is someone going to know where to send it?" he called back.

"With no address on it, I doubt it. But maybe we'll get it there someday," the voice returned.

Turning to the pile before him, the German doctor-turned-courier looked on with indecision. On one hand, he wanted to just put the letter on top of a stack and turn around and be gone. On the other, thinking of the young soldier lying on his surgical bed, asking with his dying breath for him to deliver this letter, haunted him. Holding on to the letter would do no good, either. As far as he knew, this was the only spot where he could get rid of it. Perhaps someone would track down Elizabeth, and give her the last words from her fiancé.

Henry stood in place for more than a few minutes, without interruption. His heart began to beat faster, and his mind raced as he tried to figure out what to do. He had no plans for his future. Ever so briefly he had thought of suicide, but it would take a lot more than this for his stubborn old German side to hear of that. He had nowhere to go, and nothing to do. He finally reached out his arm and placed the letter on the makeshift table, and put his empty hands in his pockets. He turned, waiting for the feeling of relief. The feeling didn't come.

"Carmen." Henry mumbled, "I miss you."

As if a length of rope was tied to his waist, he couldn't move. He faced the exit of the auditorium, expecting to leave, but couldn't. In one swift motion, he turned back to the table, picked up the letter and shoved it in his pocket.

As he strode out of the theater, the officer attending called to him, "Thank you!"

Without turning to answer, the doctor walked into the twilight. As he made his way back to the hotel, he tried not to think of anything, but he did finally have the relief he wanted to feel. The letter was a part of him now. It was the only tie to his former life, and written inside, he finally admitted, were the words that he had wished he had written to Carmen.

Chapter Thirteen

An hour or so later, he was lying in his hotel room bed, showered and shaved, with a good meal inside him. A small light sat on his bedside table, and the letter was leaning against it. As tired as he was, he could not take his eyes off of it. He wasn't sure if he had made the right decision or not, but there the letter sat anyway. It was pretty clear now, lying there, that the final request of his patient might never be fulfilled. It did make him sad, but his selfishness had won out in the long run. Yes, maybe he could go back to the theater again, and leave the letter there, but inside he knew he wouldn't do that. Maybe he'd find someone, as the war wound down, who would take it personally from him and investigate its destination. But that would mean departing with it, and for now that wasn't going to happen. Staring at the envelope, he had the desire to open it up again and read some more. Confidentiality had kept him from doing that earlier, but he had already read part of it; some more surely wouldn't hurt. Carefully lifting the white stained pages, he propped himself on his pillows, forcing his eyes to stay open and read.

I can't wait to see you sitting in the swing outside the front door, waiting for me as I arrive back home. I can smell the colourful flowers blooming in baskets around the stairs. I can hear the waves crash into the rocks way below. I think always of the day we walked on the beach hand in hand, letting the water wash over our feet. You wore that lovely blue dress with yellow buttons. I asked you to marry me that day. It's moments like those that keep me alive here. The nights are cold and damp, sleeping in abandoned churches or tents, but thinking of you warms the body and my soul. I am torn as I write, wondering if I should tell you this, but a promise made must be kept. I have some terrible news. There is no good way to tell you this, but your brother John was killed when a mortar struck our bunker and he was caught under a pile of dirt and debris. I don't think he suffered much, and I know he missed you as much as I do. We promised each other that if one of us didn't make it, the other would have to.

Henry's eyes blinked heavily, and his head dropped to his chest, as he fell asleep.

"There's a car coming." Lizzy's friend yelled out from one of the top bedrooms.

Elizabeth had been working in the garden, trying to get the stubborn soil to cooperate. It would be time to plant some seeds soon, and the ground was still hard with winter. The wind howled, as it did often on the east coast, picking up wisps of salt air on the way in.

"What's that!" she yelled back.

"A car!" her friend yelled as loud as she could, "a black car!"

Lizzy had asked her friend to stay with her for a while until her brother and fiancé came home. She didn't mind the large house all to herself, but the waiting was hard, and there certainly were enough chores to do, getting the old house back to how her brother would remember it.

Wiping some of the mud from her hands and her skirt, Elizabeth walked from the garden out back, around the side of the house, in order to see what her friend was yelling about. As she did every time a car pulled up, her heart beat faster hoping it was who she was waiting for, but the last few times, she had been sorely disappointed to only see her Pastor, who had come to check in on her. She didn't tell him that of course, but she suspected that he knew that already.

Just as she rounded the corner, the large black sedan pulled up and stopped outside her white picket fence. Shiny as if it had just been washed, the sun reflected in various places from its surface. Both rear doors opened up at the same time and the first thing she could see was legs clearly outfitted in army apparel, the familiar stripes clean and pressed.

In the next instant her emotions took her from an absolute high, to lower than rock bottom. Out of the black sedan stood two officers; clearly, not who she had expected, and now, thoroughly not who she wanted to see. With one very somber look toward her, she knew instantly why they were here.

"Carmen!" screamed Henry as he awoke from another nightmare. Henry quickly sat up in his small bed, sweat beading down his face, breathing heavily. Henry had been having more and more of these nightmares lately. Each one of them always centered on the same two things: visualizing his apartment crushing his family, and a distant, unrecognizable woman's face crying, her head buried in an unopened envelope. She would scream into the paper, shouting blame and disgust at him, until the envelope burst into flames, which then eventually consumed her. In Henry's waking world, his eyes were drawn back to the letter, which sat—which always sat—on the small mantlepiece across from his bed. It had been placed there the day he had moved in, never being touched, never being reopened.

He understood the nightmares, and why he got them, and in a sense felt that it was his punishment for the choices he had made. In fact, the nightmares of his family were the only times he thought of them. Henry wasn't a psychologist by any means, but in the back of his mind, he knew that the subject was too hard for him to think about, and as an overwhelming amount of pain will eventually cause someone to pass out into unconsciousness, so too did his conscious mind shut out memories of them so as not drive him crazy. The side effect was equally as bad, though. His heart had been hardened toward his God, himself, and his circumstance. He neither accepted companionship nor tried to seek it out. Unfortunately, his unconscious mind still leaked those lost memories during his sleep, giving him awful night terrors.

He scanned the room where he had been living for the past few years now. He had stayed in the hotel near the hospital they had arranged for him to stay for two weeks. He had tried to justify the stay by helping out the local doctors in the hospital with what remaining patients needed to be looked after, but in reality, it was because he had nowhere else to go. He told himself that he would bring the letter to someone and then move on, but he never did, and just hid it in his coat pocket. Ironically, after things had started to get back to some measure of normalcy, one of the local hospital doctors mentioned that a clinic near the outskirts of town required a doctor. It turned out the doctor there had died days before the war began, of a heart attack of all things, and the town had never replaced him, for obvious reasons. The offer was given, with the bonus of an apartment that sat on top, so without any other options, he accepted the position on the spot. The only catch was that the city landlord would come by once a month, on the first Monday, to collect some money for utilities.

He glanced at the small clock beside him; it read 5:30 a.m. Not enough time to get back to sleep, and it felt uncomfortable sleeping in damp clothes anyway. Henry washed up and ate a small breakfast and headed down the small crooked stairs to his office. With no patients expected for a few hours at least, he decided to clean up. It was always spotless of course, another habit he had picked up, but he needed to kill some time, so he cleaned it again anyway. He wore down the early morning hours without a smile on his face. He never smiled anymore. In fact, he never showed much emotion, either way. His patients had come to find him an excellent doctor, but his bedside manner had much to be desired. Calling patients in, diagnosing, and then prescribing medicine, or referring to the hospital, became mechanical to him. He accepted what little money was offered willingly, but had little use for it. He never went anywhere, save to get some food and equipment, and just hid his money in a small case under his bed.

Ding. Ding.

The small bell attached to his front door rang as the first patient of the day came in.

"Good Morning, doctor!" called the man from the front, as Henry put away the broom and dustpan, and walked out to the reception area.

The man was unknown to him.

"Can I help you?" the doctor asked somberly.

"Sorry to come so early, but the missus made me come," replied the man who wore old coveralls, and smelled like ripe fruit. "I've got this nagging sore on my elbow and she won't let me harvest our fruit until I look after it."

The fruit farmer started to unbutton his sleeve and roll up his shirt for Henry to see.

"Come in here, please."

Henry motioned, expecting the farmer to follow him into the examination room, as he turned his back and walked away. Henry opened up the door, which led to a small room with a bed, and ushered the farmer inside and started to close the door. "You know," the farmer started nervously, "I don't have much money, which is probably the reason it took so long for me to come." Henry could already tell that he would be dealing with a talker; something he wasn't looking forward to. "I was going to go to the hospital," the fruit farmer continued without much of a breath, "but they are a stickler for payment and since the war, I've been having the darndest time getting my crops to cooperate with me." Henry cut him off before he could say any more, "Let's not worry about that now, and let's take a look at your elbow."

The fruit farmer pulled his sleeve over his elbow to reveal a large red welt that showed definite signs of infection. A small patch of pus hung loosely around the wound, making it an awful sight. "It took your *wife* to make you come in for this?" questioned the doctor with no empathy. "This should have been brought to me a lot earlier, you know." The farmer sat on the bed, his face getting slightly redder, as he fumbled out an excuse. "Well like I said, we don't have much money, and...and well it didn't feel that bad until a few days ago." The doctor shook his head in unbelief, while cleaning the wound then applying some white ointment. Without giving any warning, the doctor grabbed a needle from the cabinet and drove it into the exposed shoulder of the man, making the farmer wince with pain. "Fell off the ladder, I presume," Henry asked as he dressed the wound.

"A week ago, I guess. It's harvest time for my apples." The farmer rubbed his shoulder, not sounding as chipper as he did earlier.

"Maybe you should stay away from ladders for a while then," Henry told him, not trying to sound humorous at all.

The doctor reached into his cupboard and pulled out a bottle of pills. "And take these twice a day until the bottle is empty. It will take the edge off the pain and bring down the swelling."

"Thank you, doctor, but I don't think I can afford those." The farmer rolled his sleeve back down and couldn't bring himself to grab the precious pills.

"Just take it."

Henry placed the bottle on the bed beside him and closed the cupboard, reaching over to a pad of paper that hung on the inside of the door, to write down what he had prescribed for future records. Reluctantly, and acknowledging the stiffness in his arm, the farmer grabbed the pills and hopped down, then made his way out of the examination room to the front door.

Henry followed him out but didn't feel the need to say anything else. The quietness made the farmer slightly uncomfortable as he slowed down waiting for some parting words from the doctor, which never came. "Well," the farmer said finally as he walked out the door, "I'll make sure you're paid back somehow." Henry didn't acknowledge the statement, merely turning away to the rear of the clinic, sighing heavily.

The rest of the day passed without incident. Patients came and went throughout the day, and each was dispatched in turned after being treated. It was certainly a testament to his skill that patients still came, though, as most were treated in the same fashion as the first one of the day. Finally, as the supper hour approached, Henry walked to the front door for the first time to lock up, when he saw a basket sitting to the right of the door. Reaching over, he picked up the large wicker basket, which held a dozen or so ripe green apples. Henry knew instantly why they were there, and for a very brief second, he felt he could smile, but decided not to and merely brought them inside, where he would take them upstairs to his apartment.

Day after day, night after night, Henry's life unraveled, each day seeming greyer. Every new sleep brought him an increase in the frequency of nightmares that plagued him. Often, the doctor forgot to shave in the morning, and would only remember to if one of his patients or colleagues at the hospital mentioned the scruffy state of his face. His cleanliness was always impeccable, but his looks had much to be desired. The few clothes that he owned grew holes and needed to be patched constantly. With little else to do with his time, he had decided to do that himself, which led to a less than impressive mending job. Fewer patients came to him, mostly those who knew money wouldn't be as big a factor, but many others decided to travel farther into the town to visit the hospital, where they hoped to get a more personal visit. Soon, Henry took in no more than one or two people a day and even then, worried little about it.

Even though he hadn't shown real emotion for as long as he could remember, Henry knew that he was finally drifting into depression. He could no longer hide the memories that came to him as he woke up every morning. Memories, bad memories, lingered longer and longer into each day. It took more effort to plunge them deep into his mind, somewhere that he wouldn't need to deal with them.

One morning Henry got out of bed and after eating his small breakfast, decided to go into town and fetch some supplies. He walked down the street dressed in his familiar grey woolen pants and off-white shirt. He wore a small brown hat, as the days had grown cold with summer now almost gone. His pace was slow but he felt no hurry. He glanced from side to side noticing that none of the shops were open; usually by now they would have locals streaming in and out. The air was just crisp enough to produce an ever-so-slight white puff from his mouth when he exhaled. He got a few blocks from his destination, when he heard the sound of a choir from his left. Across the street, the town church was surrounded with cars and even the occasional horse and cart combination. Standing on the opposite side of the street all alone in the crisp air, Henry heard the voices within praising his forgotten God. Only one of the large double doors stood open, still inviting those that wished to come and enter, and he could make out the heads of the congregation sitting within.

Henry stood motionless for many minutes. He wasn't sure why he was listening. The voices of farmers, merchants and their wives didn't sound altogether pleasant. The music resembled the building that it came from. It still stood on its original foundation, but one entire corner of the structure had been presumably hit by a mortar, and had been sheared off. Wooden beams and boards had been hammered in place to keep the elements out, but it still needed a lot of work—much like the tune the choir tried to carry. Finally, the music came to a close and Henry listened to the choir settle down. A single male voice began to speak from inside. It would be the preacher, Henry surmised. The air around Henry was still; there was no wind or rain, no traffic or people disturbed him. He was alone on his island across from where the word of God was about to be preached. He could hear the voice as if it was inside his head, when in fact it was pretty distant and quiet. No amplification was being used, but the preacher somehow projected it to Henry's ears.

"And we continue with our reading this morning from Romans, chapter eight, verse twenty-eight." The preacher cleared his throat unusually loudly. "'And we know that God causes all things to work together for good to those who love God, to those who are called according to His purpose.' Isn't that a wonderful promise, folks?"

Henry stood listening, oblivious of whatever else was going on around him.

"We all want to know what's going on, don't we?" the preacher continued, "But God sometimes keeps things hidden from us, and we just need to trust in him. Trust that He knows what He's doing."

"Crackpot," Henry whispered loudly, realizing that he had crept closer to the building, now standing just outside the broken church. His harsh word caused a few people in the very rear of the church to look back sternly. Henry didn't care.

"Isn't it funny, how we grow to love God in times of plenty, times when our crops are good and the body feels fine," continued the Preacher. "But when troubles come our way, we turn and flee. Most times cursing God on our way out."

"Crackpot," Henry said again loudly, finally having heard enough. Once again faces turned to him, in an attempt to get him to quiet down, without actually saying anything.

He knew the verse the preacher had referenced. While not a learned biblical scholar, Henry had memorized Bible verses in his youth, as most Anglican or Catholic children did when they were young. It sounded like a slap on the face to him. After all he'd been through so far, God wanted him to trust Him.

Henry turned to the direction he was originally headed, and then stopped. Looking toward his destination and then back at the church, he clued in to the fact that it must be Sunday. He hadn't even bothered to check, and of course the stores wouldn't be open today. Something inside him allowed the emotional pendulum of his circumstances to finally swing to the far side. He swung his body around, feeling more depressed than he had ever before. Walking back to his home, his head hung as low as it could.

His feet shuffled on the cracked cement, kicking up loose dust and rocks. His heart sank with each footstep. Life had been hard admittedly; his lack of family and of friends had always been able to be put off with his work. His dedication to his profession had kept his mind occupied for the most part. Thinking of the last few years, he knew that he could have been more empathetic to his patients, but the quality of care was unsurpassed. He took pride in that. Couldn't everyone see that? Why did everyone hate him so much? It didn't seem to matter anymore. There were no more patients, or very few. He didn't want to think of Carmen and Eden, Egon and Else, the captain and his son, the elderly couple who lost their son, with death in its full magnitude lying beneath their balcony.

"They're all dead," Henry muttered, repeating the words the old lady had told him. "They're all dead." Repeating the line over and over again, Henry found himself in his empty room standing beside his bed. He had no recollection of the steps he had taken to get here. "Everyone I know is gone," he continued. "I have no one left."

The German doctor's mind couldn't be budged this time. He could only focus on the pain and misery he had seen and endured. With a blank face, almost as a corpse, he allowed his mind to dwell on the worst.

Without pausing to reflect on what he was about to do, he found some rope in the closet opposite the front door. It was old and cracked, but that didn't matter. It probably hadn't seen the light of day for years, but it was rope, and that was all that mattered. He climbed the bed and reached up to one of the roof beams that ran the length of his apartment. With some effort he was able to shove the rope above it and under the wooden ceiling, and fasten a knot. With the other end he made a small loop and crammed it around his neck, not bothering to even test if it would hold him or not. Standing on the bed looking down, he envisioned himself walking off the bed and to his doom. He wanted the end to come quick, he thought. "I have nothing." Henry said, finally standing on the corner of the bed with only a short step between this pain and the next.

He closed his eyes and took in the full memory of his family and their last times together. He let all the memories he had tried to suppress flood through him like an unyielding wave. He refused to show any emotion, but took the barrage, as a soldier would fists and muzzles, in close combat. No tears ran from his cheeks. He wouldn't let them. He was still too angry for that to happen, but wanted to finish his days remembering his loved ones, no matter how hard that would be. He owed it to them. Each new memory hit him harder than the last, as he stood on the bed with his eyes tightly shut. "I have nothing," Henry said again, opening his eyes, ready to end the pain.

He gingerly took a small step, letting one foot dangle from the bed, with the other ready to follow. His arms folded on his chest, unsure of where exactly to put them.

In the instant before he took the final step, his eyes opened wide. Across the room, still sitting on the mantelpiece, was the letter. That white familiar envelope staring at him, almost as if calling out to him. Henry could hear the words it was telling him. He could hear the words sear into his brain, yelling at him, pleading with him. His other foot slid from the bed, as the momentum of his body pushed him forward, dropping him down, as the small slack in the rope tightened.

God causes all things to work together for good, Henry remembered it in that instant. Just as the rope had no more slack, Henry shot up his arms, desperately reaching up to grab hold. He felt it tighten hard on his neck, but he had at least absorbed the snap of the rope. He heard the creak of the old rope rub against his throat, as pain shot up to his head, and then down to his toes. There was no open passage inside his throat to take in more air, but Henry held the rope fast above his head hoping to stop what he had foolishly done. Henry's eyes blurred and his room started to lose colour and contrast. In a final attempt, he pulled on the rope with what little strength he had left.

"*God, please.*" he thought, without thinking.

As the lights went out, the last things he heard were the snap of the rope and the sound of his head hitting the floor.

Chapter Fourteen

"Missing!" Elizabeth shrieked, "What do you mean missing?" She stood on the porch with her friend holding her as best she could, as Lizzy shook uncontrollably.

"I'm sorry, Ma'am." The unfortunate officer repeated, "We mean that we can't find him."

"Did you look for him?" she shot back.

"Of course, for several weeks in fact." the other officer continued, standing perfectly still in full uniform. "He never reported to his commanding officer, or to his unit for that matter. No one else has seen or heard from him since shortly before the war ended." Lizzy paused, tears rolling down her face uncontrollably. Her friend took the opportunity to guide her to a seat and have her sit down. The two officers remained standing, and cast worried looks at each other, with all-too-familiar sorrow in their eyes.

"First you tell me that my brother is dead, and now you say my husband is missing." Lizzy wasn't pleased, to say the least.

"Fiancé you mean, right?" one of the soldiers asked mistakenly.

"He would have been my husband!" she yelled at them. "What am I to do now?"

Lizzy buried her face in her hands and cried.

"Again, I am so sorry," one of the soldiers added, "we will try to locate him, but I'm afraid if we can't we will have to declare him permanently missing from action."

"Dead, you mean?" Elizabeth asked, her voice cracking under the strain.

"Yes, ma'am."

Henry opened his eyes to pain. Before noticing where he was, he felt the pain surround and penetrate his neck. It felt as if a clamp was placed around his neck, holding it far too tight. His eyes adjusted to the light and he could tell from the familiar colours that he was in a hospital room. Beside him the rustle of another patient behind a curtain confirmed it. He had been here before, but looking down on the beds like the one he now occupied. Taking time to let his vision get back to normal, Henry tried to prop himself up on his elbows, but blood rushed to his head and the queasiness forced him to drop back down on his pillow, sending a twinge of pain from his neck. After a few minutes a nurse came by, as she did her usual rounds, when she saw Henry with his eyes opened up. She strode over, smiling down at him adjusting the pillow under his head. He recognized her, but couldn't place her.

"Doctor," the nurse exclaimed. "It is good to see you, awake."

Henry opened his mouth to talk but couldn't. Even trying sent a surge of pain to his throat.

"Don't bother, Doctor." The nurse understood what he was trying to do. "You won't be able to talk for a while, and you'll have a nasty scar there for a long time. Here you go."

The nurse took paper and a pen from his bedside in the anticipation that he would need to communicate. Henry stared at the primitive form of communication, then back to the nurse, his eyes keeping her at his bedside. He felt exhausted for someone that had just gotten up a few minutes ago, but only one thing was on his mind now, and he wouldn't be able to sleep until he put his plans in motion. With a few belabored strokes, he wrote down two simple words: *my letter*. Feeling drained, he then put the pen down and closed his eyes.

For the first time in months, his nightmares were held at bay. Determination and relief staved off other depressing thoughts. His dreams centered only on the letter, and at one point he even envisioned the same unrecognizable woman grasping the letter. Just before the dream faded the woman began opening the envelope, and turned to Henry smiling. It would be another twenty hours before Henry opened his eyes again. This time the room was silent and the only light was the pale glow from the moon outside his window. With a twang from his stomach, Henry uncomfortably swung his whole body sideways, unable to rotate his neck on its own, and looked down at the bedside table. Sitting on it was a small plate of fruit with a glass of water beside it. But more importantly was the all-too-familiar edges and creases of the stained letter, sitting in its envelope. It gave him comfort just to see it there. A funny emotion set over him, a feeling of peace, and of purpose. He grabbed the letter with the one hand that could reach, and held it close to his chest. This would be his mission. He would find out who Elizabeth was and bring it to her. Not some anonymous postal carrier. Not an English soldier that didn't care about the contents. He would do it himself. He would do it, because no one else could. "If God couldn't give me the purpose I needed," he muttered almost silently, and with much pain, "then I will find it myself. I don't need God. You can't stop me this time." Henry held the letter at his breast for a long time, smiling an almost evil grin, at the confidence he had in himself. He could do this, he thought.

He ate a few of the fruits and drank some of the water offered, feeling the lack of nourishment within him, but he drew sustenance from the paper that rubbed close to him. His mind began to process what little information he had already, which was admittedly not much. He wondered how exactly he would find Elizabeth. Other than being the woman of an English soldier, probably a Canadian soldier, there wasn't much to go on. It didn't matter, though; he would find her somehow. After all it was his destiny, and his alone.

Henry ate and drank slowly, feeling the burning sensation as it passed down to his stomach. Eating and drinking while lying on the bed proved quite difficult. He took his time, feeling much better emotionally, if not physically, than he had in a long time.

It was several hours before the night nurse came around to check on her patients.

"You're up I see." She noticed Henry gazing about. "Had a good sleep?"

Henry nodded, not bothering to attempt to speak.

"I would think so, you slept nearly a day," she exclaimed. "You're the doctor from town, aren't you?"

Henry nodded again. Without asking, the nurse brushed away some fruit peels that had lodged themselves in the bed sheets, and grabbed her patient from the back, propping him up with another pillow.

"Did you enjoy the food?" she asked.

Again, Henry nodded.

"It was a gift from the day nurse. She says she remembered you from a few years back, at the end of the war. She is worried about you."

Henry stared at her, finally placing the face in his mind.

Without much tact, the nurse said, "There is a rumour going around that you tried to kill yourself."

Henry turned his face as best as he could, not wanting to look at her anymore.

"That's okay," she stated somewhat empathetically. "We all have rough spots. The important part is that you're all right."

Henry didn't turn back, waiting for the nurse to lose interest.

"Well," she said, finally accepting the doctor wasn't in a *talking* mood. "God bless, and I hope you feel better soon.

After a few uncomfortable minutes of no more interaction, deliberately on Henry's part, the nurse finally walked away.

"I'll feel better, don't worry, "Henry thought, "God won't have anything to do with it."

Chapter Fifteen

THE CRESCENT PALE moon cast an eerie glow through the living room windows, giving a dim white-blue shimmer to Elizabeth's face. She sat in her familiar chair, rocking slowly back and forth, creaking slowly like a cat whose tail was gently being tugged. Her knitting needles were cast on the floor beside her. In fact, she hadn't picked them up for a long time now. Even during her sporadic cleaning sprees, she had never picked them up, always hoping that it would be to news her fiancé was found and on his way home. She sat with bags under her eyes, unable to sleep. In one hand rested her Bible, the other a glass of gin. She had never been much of a drinker, but lately found some ill-fated comfort in the bottle. Lizzy took a slow sip of the burning liquid and pursed her lips as it went down. She stared out the window, past the falling fence posts, toward the driveway, always hoping but somehow never believing.

It had been a while now since the news had reached her. Her friend had tried to get her to come to grips with the news. Lizzy knew she wanted her to put Alan and John behind her, but she couldn't do that. Not yet. It was becoming too hard to have her around, so she asked her to leave, and let her be. It took several weeks but her long-time friend finally relented. She had her own life to lead, and promised to stop by once in a while to check up on her. The visits came as promised, but soon the frequency of them diminished. Her pastor and members of the congregation stopped by as well, helping her with some chores, bringing her food and tending to some of her household needs. But with the lack of appreciation and the smell of alcohol, even those visits became less frequent. Her pastor remained faithful though, and made a point to stop by once a week to make sure nothing drastic had happened.

The last time he was here, he had told her, "He's been missing for a while now, Elizabeth. Maybe it's time to let go."

"Never," she thought as he spoke. "He's missing, not dead. He could come home any time."

The pastor was a kind man, she knew, but he wouldn't sway her. He could still be alive. He had to be. Before the pastor left, he had taken her family Bible out of the desk, and opened it up to a passage he had wanted her to think about for a while. Now she sat in the chair her father had made so many years ago, thinking about what it said. She couldn't let go of him. He was her life. He promised her that he would come home. Where was he? "God, bring him back to me," she prayed silently. "Tell me where he is." She closed her eyes, not bothering to wipe away the tears that trickled down her cheek, tickling her nose. She fell asleep again in her chair, with her fingers still holding the spot in the book where she was reading.

'And we know that in all things God works for the good of those who love him, who have been called according to his purpose'.

Henry stayed in his hospital room for the next few days before being released. He was anxious to get out, but used his time lying in bed or wandering the hallways trying to ask questions about his future destination. He knew Canada existed, but that was about all. When he found out that it was situated right above America, he was surprised. To think that it even stretched the entire length of America was even more surprising. One of the doctors he had questioned, had traveled to the eastern United States many years before, luckily getting out of there a year or so before the war began, and remembered hearing about Canada. He told Henry what he had learned of Vancouver, Saskatchewan, Toronto and Montreal. Surprisingly, even though living so close, most Americans, the other doctor found, didn't know much about Canada. They did know it was cold and vast.

Henry wasn't much of a conversationalist, but gave more effort than he had in a long time to talk as best he could, with the help of pen and paper, to the nurses and doctors, and even the odd patient. He had been fortunate to talk to an ex-soldier from Britain who had stayed in town after the war. He had been shot several times in the back, and while he was very fortunate to have lived and more miraculously walked, he did require constant checkups and rehabilitation to check on his damaged spine. The added bonus of falling in love with a German nurse made his stay a permanent one. He had felt some pain in his back lately, and his new wife had made him come in for an extended checkup. John Moxon was his name. A former tank gunner for the 32nd, he had said. He did know more about Canada than anyone else Henry had talked to, for what that was worth. "Something about it being in the great commonwealth," Henry thought.

He described the western Rockies to the prairies, and all the way to the eastern shores of Nova Scotia. He was a talkative man, throwing in stories of his military career, and trips to all parts of the world. Henry continued attempts to steer the conversation back to Canada, and had asked if he knew where Elizabeth lived, which drew a great belly laugh from the man. Canada was a huge country, the Brit had chuckled, "I've only been there once, and I couldn't possibly know everyone." Henry had sat on a chair by his bed, trying to hide the redness in his face. "How would I get there then?" Henry had replied, trying to get to the meat of the matter. Apparently, he was told, you could go by plane, but it was an expensive proposition. A boat seemed the logical way, the ex-soldier offered.

Henry had gotten into more than he wanted, having to listen to this jovial man start up another story about his self-described wonderful and exotic life. Henry wondered how his wife dealt with him, although maybe he had found an ear in Henry where he didn't have one at home. With one last try, and just before Henry claimed fake pain and discomfort in order to escape, he learned that Hamburg was his best bet for a way out of Europe and towards Canada. Realizing that he wasn't going to get much more useful information, Henry just turned himself over with a grunt, and stopped talking. It took the Brit a few more sentences to figure out the conversation was over, and with an oblivious chuckle, walked away in his green hospital gown to find another ear.

Within a week of being back at his apartment, the pain in his throat eased. He was able to talk more lucidly, albeit slowly, and with a lot less discomfort. He took in no more patients at his clinic and decided he wouldn't be able to concentrate enough; the fact that there were barely one or two a day, made his decision easier. A simple call to the landlord would put in motion the decision to either call another doctor in, or just close the clinic down for good.

Late one evening he finally gathered the courage to pack his bags in anticipation and got himself into bed well after midnight. Henry stared at his own reflection in the dim light of a single lamp, looking at the scar in his throat that wrapped almost entirely from one end to the other. Stroking it gently, feeling the ripples of skin under his fingers, he grew excited. "I'm going to do it," Henry told himself. "I'm really going to do it." He shivered with excitement, eager to have something real and tangible to cling to for once in a long while. The German doctor reached under his bed and pulled out the small wooden box he kept all his money in. He would call the bus company first thing in the morning and book a ride to Hamburg.

It had been a full agonizing two days later, but now Henry sat near the back looking out the window of a bus that would take him to Hamburg. The trip would take far too long, with one overnight stay, as it would weave in and out of the highways picking up and dropping off passengers on the way. Most of the major arteries of the country were fixed and re-paved, but many smaller byways still required slow passage due to the damage wrought upon them.

The sun was shining in a bright blue sky, and even with the outside temperatures low, the heat of the large orange sun warmed Henry's face. Sitting beside him was a young man, probably in his late thirties, looking all too eager to start up a conversation. Henry felt cursed, seemingly drawing conversationalists to him. He was dressed in a nice suit, one that looked as if had been worn more than a few times, but taken care of.

Henry tried desperately not to look at him, as the bus bounced along one of the roads that would lead them to another drop-off point. It was getting hard to just stare out the window hour after hour, and with the bus lurching to and fro, taking a nap was out of the question.

"So, mister." Henry anticipated the obvious question. "Where are you going?"

Henry continued to stare out the window, hoping the man would think he was asleep or at least deep in thought. The bus hit a large pothole, sending all the passengers including the two in row ten, up almost off their seats and then back down with a thud.

"Sorry!" yelled the driver.

"Nice bit of road, eh?" Henry's riding companion chirped up again, not able to believe he could have slept through that.

Henry glanced over ever so briefly and smiled as best as he could, to at least acknowledge the man in hopes that he would mind his own business. Henry's eyes met his, and then noticed them squint slightly as they dropped to the large scar on his throat. Henry turned back to the window, placing his hand over his neck and rubbing the scar slightly.

Curiosity was setting in deeply with the young man, and there would be no silencing him now.

"I'm heading as far as Frankfurt, what about you?" he chirped cheerfully.

"Hamburg," Henry stated, calculating the amount of time it would take to get there in his mind.

"Hamburg, huh," the man piped. "Been there a few times myself. Nice place. Got some business there?"

Henry sighed, wanting the brief conversation to be over already.

"Taking a boat to Canada," Henry replied eventually.

"Wow. Over to Canada, huh. That must be exciting. Are you there on business or pleasure?"

Henry placed a hand on his breast pocket feeling the letter against his chest.

"Visiting a friend," Henry told him, thinking that it was somewhat the truth.

"I'm heading to Frankfurt, trying to get a job at Mercedes," the man continued, oblivious to Henry's lack of enthusiasm. "I hear they are looking for a few managers there."

Again, Henry smiled, this time not even bothering to turn around. The young man tried to start the conversation up again a few times, but finally gave into the fact that it would be a one-way street. Within minutes, the bus came to a stop behind a small restaurant, and opened up its doors.

"Twenty-minute stop folks!" the driver yelled out. "Back in your seats by one o'clock."

"I'll have to find a different seat, that's for sure." Henry mumbled quietly.

Don't worry Lizzy. I'll come back home soon. I hope to come back soon. Halifax seems a long way from the ditches of Germany but I can see myself there every time I dream of you. I dream for Nova Scotia and for you, every time I see a burned out building or a scorched farm field. Yesterday I sat in my bunker with a man from Toronto. He had a picture of his wife and three children in his coat. I could see the love he had for them whenever he took out the old stained photograph. He tells me that he wants to have more children. He talks about them all the time, and every time he does, I just think of you. I want to have children with you. I want to be a dad to ten boys and five girls. I want to give you everything that you have been missing since I've been gone. I want to feel the warmth of your skin pressed against mine. I will one day soon, make the trip back over the ocean to be with you again.

Henry pressed the letter close to him as he read it some more sitting on the bus as it rumbled closer to Hamburg.

"Nova Scotia," he confirmed in his mind. "Halifax, Nova Scotia.

That must be where Elizabeth lives. He felt good about himself. He could do this all by himself, where no one else could. He felt a little like the detectives he had read about in books when he was little, solving the mystery with nothing but their wits to guide them. He had read more of the letter as he rode in the bus on the second day. The bus had finally pulled into Frankfurt late that evening, and he had slept in a small room provided by the ticket agent. It was with pleasure he had seen the young man disappear in the night, as he dreamed of work in an auto manufacturing plant.

He would arrive in Hamburg in the early afternoon, with not as many stops as the day before. Luckily for him, the seat next to him was empty and the time flew by more pleasantly, enjoying another bright day outside and dreaming of embarking over the ocean to meet Elizabeth. It seemed as if his journey were almost at an end already. With only a few more hours to Hamburg, a ride across the Atlantic, and then merely to find Elizabeth in Nova Scotia. How difficult could that be, he thought?

Chapter Sixteen

TIME FLEW BY, as the road disappeared behind the bus as it cruised along the German highway. He thought of Elizabeth. What she would look like? How would she react to him bringing her the letter? She would undoubtedly give him a hero's welcome.

"I mean, to come all that way to deliver her late fiancé's last testament to her, should be worth something," he thought to himself. Henry envisioned her arms wrapped around him and holding him tight, tears running down her face. He could feel the warmth of her breath on his ear, and the beating of her heart against his. He pulled her back ever so gently in his daydream, to look at her reassuringly. Instead of an imaginary face, he was now looking into the warm glance of Carmen. He closed his eyes even tighter, as his head leaned against the bus window. He longed for that warmth that Carmen gave him with every nod, every smile, every hug, and every kiss. He held the beautiful memory for a few seconds longer, letting the image wash over him. His face grew cold, leaning on the window, which despite the bright sun, had cooled and now left a slight film of moisture on his cheek. Henry let his eyes open slowly, adjusting again to the light, realizing how much more this trip meant to him than it possibly was to Elizabeth. Looking outside, cars drew alongside the bus and then past it, oblivious to his important journey, only concerned with their own daily routines. Town after town swept by and with the last stop finally behind him, he could hardly wait to get off, and get to his next step.

As if to affirm his eagerness, the bus came to a final stop an hour earlier than expected. Henry rubbed his bottom as he disembarked from the bus, out onto another platform with another familiar restaurant behind it. He retrieved his baggage, which consisted of a single small suitcase, and made for the tiny portable ticket booth erected near the end of the bus. An elderly gentleman dressed in an oversized blue suit stood there already, dispensing passes to waiting customers. A small number of people were trying to buy return tickets south, as Henry stroked the letter in his breast pocket for reassurance.

With his impatience starting to show, Henry finally found himself at the front of the line.

"Can I help you?" the ticket man asked.

"Yes." Henry replied, "one ticket to Canada."

The man in the ticket window stared at him confused.

"Canada?" the old ticket man asked curiously.

"Nova Scotia, actually, I think it's in Canada," Henry stated with purpose.

There was an uneasy moment of silence as the ticket agent stared at Henry, trying to figure out what exactly he was being asked. Henry was a smart man. He studied hard and had become a fine doctor, but geography was never his passion, let alone international geography. He knew that Canada wasn't a short bus ride from here, but he didn't think this might be more complicated than he had thought. Or at least he didn't think that far ahead to plan on how he was going to get from here to there.

"You're looking to get into Canada, then?"

"That's what I said. Nova Scotia, Canada. One ticket please."

"I can't sell you a ticket to Canada, mister." The ticket agent chuckled under his breath with unbelief, seeing the seriousness of the question.

Henry didn't respond, feeling the air of discomfort extend beyond him. A young couple behind him in the line added their own chuckles, listening in on the conversation.

"I can take you to the port though," the old man in the makeshift podium added. "There will be a bus along shortly that can take you down there. From there you can ask about getting yourself to Canada."

Looking briefly at the young couple behind him, and seeing their amused faces, Henry faced the agent with embarrassment.

"Ok. I'll go there."

Henry reached into his small purse and as quickly as he could, paid for the short ride.

Within a few hours he was standing in another lineup, rubbing his buttocks, in front of a completely different ticket window. This one was a permanent structure, and housed a middle-aged woman who was dispensing tickets to singles, couples, and family travelers. The line moved slowly, allowing Henry's aches to migrate from his buttocks to his legs. People in front of him were passing papers back and forth, and filling out documents. Henry glanced beyond the ticket window to the large building behind it. It was an ominous structure, housing the multitude of travelers waiting to leave and those that were returning. A few large ships could be seen resting gently on the calm waters behind it. People walked to and fro around the building, mostly carrying luggage and holding their loved ones in their arms. The scene took Henry back to better times along the Rhine. The water wasn't as vast, and the ships were a lot smaller, but the smell and sounds felt the same. Henry closed his eyes while waiting and took in the ambiance, taking him back to his days when he lived near the water. Before he could let any memories seep into his mind, he opened his eyes, refusing to daydream. He told himself he didn't want to remember anything like that again. He did it far too often. The quickening of his heart gave him all the reason not to allow his emotions to drag him back to the eventual destruction he was trying to forget.

"No more tears, Henry," he told himself. "I won't give God the satisfaction."

He finally walked to the ticket window and with some hesitation, he asked, "One ticket to Canada."

With no sign of repeating his previous humiliation, the woman flipped through some pages.

"Canada," she paused. "First stop Halifax, Nova Scotia, and then on to…?"

"Halifax, yes, that's where I want to go. Perfect." Henry smiled devilishly.

"Three hundred marks. Passenger deck. Four hundred marks first class, one way."

Henry looked shocked.

"Three hundred marks?" Henry asked. "That's pretty expensive."

He looked into his money purse, quickly determining that he wouldn't have enough.

"Three hundred marks," Henry repeated to himself, feeling angry. "I don't have that much."

Henry's heart sank. He hadn't even thought that he wouldn't have enough money. After the bus trip, the overnight hotels and all the meals, he didn't think to conserve his marks to that extent.

Henry's hands started shaking; instinctively searching in his pockets for some loose change, if that would make a difference. Unfortunately, when he felt the letter folded gently in his pocket, it made his heart sink even further. He could feel the irritation on the faces of the people behind him in line. Henry looked back at the ticket lady with a blank stare, hoping for a reprieve from the large amount. It was immediately apparent that it wouldn't come.

Making a quick count of what he had, he drew in a large breath.

"Two hundred and ten marks. That's all I've got."

The ticket lady stared back, took a deep breath of indifference, and then reached under the counter for another binder.

"When do you need to get there?" she asked, staring at the pages in the binder.

"I just want to get there," Henry told her desperately. "I need to get there."

Henry stiffened his back just a bit in determination, maybe hoping that his demeanor would show her how important this was to him.

"There might be a chance, hang on one second." The ticket agent thumbed through the binder, running her finger up and down one particular page, finding a number and then dialing the same on the phone beside her.

"Do you have a transport to Canada?" the lady asked on the phone. After a short pause she continued, "When? Ok, thank you. Yes, I'll make sure he hurries up."

Replacing the phone back in its receiver, the ticket lady turned back to Henry.

"There is a transport leaving for Canada. I'm afraid it is leaving today. In fact, it's leaving in a few hours; seems you got lucky, if you can make it. It is one hundred eighty-five marks."

Henry's pulse quickened with excitement.

"Thank you. Thank you." Henry reached into his wallet and pulled out the remainder of his money. Counting out enough cash, the ticket lady recounted and wrote some information in the binder.

"I'm afraid the accommodations won't be very luxurious."

Henry nodded, barely listening, smiling at his luck.

"Do you have your papers?" she asked as she printed out Henry's name on a small ticket and stamped it.

"Papers?" Henry asked.

"Papers. Passport. Documentation."

In all his planning, which now in hindsight didn't seem well thought out, he hadn't figured on the fact that all his personal belongings had been lost during the war. Sitting somewhere in his destroyed building laid the remains of his life on paper. He had served in the war, survived the war. He had healed those in need, and had buried the dead. He even attempted to start a new life, all without the need of proof of who he was.

Henry glanced at the women behind the glass and timidly told her, "I don't have any."

Surprisingly the lady didn't press the point.

"Well the transport isn't a civilian ship per se. You'll have to take it up with them when you get there. Mostly military cargo, that couldn't wait for an official transport. There are a few stray passengers, mostly for those that need to travel along with it, but some like yourself that simply can't afford a proper journey. Henry took the ticket given to him, gladly not letting himself get worried about the details.

"It leaves in an hour or so and you'll need to walk a mile or so to Pier Three. Good luck, they'll be shutting down the gate soon," She added, already ushering over the couple that were impatiently waiting behind him.

Henry scanned the area behind the ticket booths, which was a lot larger than he had thought. He could make out a few huge ships docked in the distance and surmised that one of them had to be his. A large billboard sat a few feet away, with a simple map attached. The route didn't seem difficult, so he started out as quickly as he could. Passing a few coffee stands made his stomach rumble, but his dwindling money and the lack of time forced him to continue on. After half an hour of peering through warehouse windows, and fumbling with locked doors, Henry finally spotted the ramp in the distance, attached to an old cargo ship waiting for him on the still waters.

Henry made a beeline to the ramp, wondering why there was so little activity at the dock. Other than a few forklifts and dock personnel moving to and fro, the dock looked empty. A uniformed army officer stood at the base of the ramp, sorting some papers. He picked up a phone sitting beside the ramp, and waved his arms as he talked. Immediately a loud churning could be heard from the old ship, and the ramp started to lift.

"Hello!" Henry screamed, picking up his pace considerably.

The dock officer turned to the voice.

"I have a ticket, wait!" the hopeful passenger cried again.

The officer crooked his head slightly, watching the last passenger run in desperation toward him, and then picked up the phone. As Henry's stride turned into a full sprint, the ramp creaked to a halt, but remained in place. Within a minute, Henry pulled up to the young man in uniform, panting heavily.

"I…have…a ticket…here." He pulled out the paper from his coat pocket and placed it in the man's hand.

"The ship is leaving now; you'll have to jump from the ramp to the ship platform." The man grabbed the ticket and threw Henry's small pack up the few feet from the ramp. It wasn't a big gap, but Henry with a renewed sense of purpose and determination, found an inner energy as if he was almost crossing the entire ocean in this small gap, and felt like he had leapt across like a gazelle. But in reality, Henry jumped as high as he could and with a grunt landed like an old and less athletic gazelle, then lifted himself up from the landing and brushed off the rust and dirt.

"Do you have your papers?" the man waiting at the other end of the ramp asked him, as if it was simply a formality.

Henry didn't answer, hoping in his silence he could pretend he couldn't hear. His heart beat faster, desperately worrying if his trip would come to an abrupt end. "Did they check it at the front of the ramp?" the ship officer asked, seemingly unaware of proper procedure, and probably not caring very much. "Yes!" Henry yelled back, already creeping forward to the ship along the steel ramp, hoping his answer would suffice. He felt guilty lying, but he thought that it really wasn't a lie, as they did check if he had his papers at the first ticket booth. Without even responding, the officer nodded and picked up the phone one last time. He waited for Henry to scurry past him and make the final few steps from the edge of the ship to the solid landing, before giving the all clear to continue retracting the large steel ramp. Sweat beaded from Henry's forehead, barely believing he had successfully made it aboard.

Henry stood at the edge of the ship watching the ramp retract, grinning proudly as he had all on his own found passage to his destination. In fact, he couldn't believe his luck. It was only a few days prior he was sitting on his bed wondering if he could actually do it. Wondering if he could do what he knew no other person could. He smiled proudly to himself, as the ship finally let go a blast of its horn that would have woken the dead, and pushed its way from the dock and toward the open ocean. Holding the rail and letting the breeze caress his face, he reached for the letter and stroked it gently, letting its presence build his confidence even more. Looking up to the sky, the now-retired German doctor squinted in the sun, and paid no homage to whom he thought was up there, somewhere. This was his mission. His time. He would find purpose in this journey. Purpose no one else could give him.

Dust clung to the open pages of the Bible that sat next to Elizabeth; open to the passage she had read before, and hadn't touched since. The living room, in which Lizzy sat, smelled like an abandoned warehouse. The windows hadn't been opened in a terribly long time, even on beautiful sunny days. The air was still brisk outside, and the wind brushed against the single-paned glass, as if asking to come in. Lizzy ignored it. Alcohol reeked on her breath. She was more often drunk than she was sober, and her attitude and temperament showed clearly in what state she was in now. When not loafing around in the house, she would take short walks in her tattered bed robe around the property, her unstable mind waiting to hear the sounds of a particular car engine, one which had never come.

Today, however, she sat in her old chair sipping her first gin of the morning. Her head still rang from the night before, and a small drink, she figured, would settle it down nicely. Glasses were strewn around the house, left idle in every nook and cranny, most with little remnants of alcohol left inside. With the windows shut tight, Elizabeth sat in her favorite spot and took a slow small sip, glancing at the dirty glass and beyond it, as one would at something hated and loved at the same time. Lizzy glanced over to the foyer, across the room, to where a yellow rope was hanging. Lizzy stared at it for what seemed an eternity. Minutes dragged by as the liquid in the glass was disappearing, much like her sobriety, and the yellow cord swayed ever so slightly in the musty air. It was something she had planned out in her drunken stupor the night before. She had thrown the rest of her glass of bad scotch across the room and screamed to the sky. Her husband wasn't coming home, was he? Her brother had been lost long ago, but for the first time she felt she had just lost her husband. All those terrible years of not admitting it. Of denying it. Of telling everyone that cared for her that they were wrong and there was still a chance that he would be coming back. It all crashed down on her yesterday evening as she strung the rope she had found in the shed to the railing above the foyer. She stared at it for long hours, as more of the toxic liquid entered her system. She had leaned over and coughed repeatedly, feeling the vibrations right inside her body. It was only the fact that she had no balance and was intoxicated to a huge degree that she didn't follow up with her plans. Collapsing on the floor, she was spared at least for the moment from an end to her miserable life. But it was now morning, and the rope still hung, casting a long skinny shadow on the staircase behind it. Her head rang like a church bell, but it was clearer than it had been for a long time, which didn't say much.

She walked slowly up the stairs thinking that this would be the best way to end her life. She had spent most of her savings on booze, and short of selling her house, had little left financially. Her stomach rumbled for the lack of food, and with a rub of her chest felt the ribs that were beginning to show through the skin. Soon there would be no more telephone service or heat, and the house would be devoid of life completely.

Lizzy climbed the stairs with the almost-empty glass in one hand, and the other caressing the railing. Reaching the top, she breathed heavily and looked down to the foyer with apprehension, yet with a strange sensation of excitement. If her beloved were truly dead, this would be the only way to find him, and for him to find her. Another round of repeated coughs made her dizzy and she had to grasp the railing with both hands, letting the glass in her hand fall to the floor below with a loud crash, sending glass fragments and brown liquid everywhere.

"Alan," Lizzy whimpered. "You're really dead, aren't you?"

Elizabeth let the tears run from her eyes unabated.

"Who is going to take care of me now?"

The desperate woman stared over the railing, ready to end her existence, when the door below her came to life with a knock.

Lizzy's pulse jumped, as she had the brief idea that this was finally the visit she was hoping for.

Knock. Knock.

The knock sounded again, louder this time.

Lizzy stood on the second floor with both hands still on the railing, wanting to run down to open the door, but feared it would be another disappointment.

"Elizabeth!" a voice screamed from outside.

It was the pastor.

Elizabeth peered down again to the floor of the foyer, ready to jump, fully realizing that her husband-to-be was dead, and never coming home. There would be no more denials. She wouldn't, couldn't deny it any more.

"Elizabeth!" Again, the familiar voice from the other side of the door beckoned her. "I know you're in there. Are you all right?"

Lizzy sighed and looked to her hand, hoping there would still be a drink in it. As a knock came from the door one more time, she turned her head to the side and let go another round of intense coughs, feeling her head swim. With one swoop of her head she saw the ceiling above her, noticing ever so briefly the cracks in the white paint, and then everything went blurry and she felt her feet give way as her body tilted and fell towards the stairs. The last thing she felt was her shoulder and head hit the third stair from the top. Funny, though, that she didn't feel any pain.

Chapter Seventeen

A TINY ROOM WITH hardly enough room to spread his legs was all that one hundred and eighty-five marks paid for. The cabin, if you could call it that, came with the most basic of amenities. A wooden plank, with a few sheets thrown on top for a bed, and a shelf made of bricks and old steel. This ship was no cruise liner. His cabin was mid-ship, three decks down, in a long hallway that held all the freighter's living quarters. Most were near the same size as his, but certainly none of them smaller. He guessed that with the late ticket purchase, and the low cost, it was all he was going to get. Even food was hard to come by. There was a cafeteria one level up, which served meals three times a day, but the food wasn't very good. Henry couldn't understand how the military functioned on such food. Granted, this was a private vessel, but he would have figured any country that sent their soldiers to a foreign soil to fight would at least be given proper food to eat. Half-cooked eggs, powdered milk and the odd scrap piece of ham were parts of the illustrious menu this ship had to offer.

Henry spent most of the time walking on the upper deck, watching the white waves crash against the side and slide backwards, leaving Henry to follow with his eyes as far as he could. There weren't many people on the ship, at least that he could see. 'Restricted' signs draped various doors, leading him to believe there could be more people somewhere, but he couldn't find them. It was clear this ship was primarily carrying military personnel, with uniformed officers walking back and forth tending to whatever duties they had. From talking to the cafeteria worker, Henry learned that it was still a privately owned vessel, but was being used mostly to carry military vehicles and equipment back to Canada and the United States. Mostly nonessential equipment and personnel that couldn't wait, or didn't want to, until the next army-supply ship, that sailed the same route at a later date.

As Henry stood upon the deck, one of the uniformed officers walked past, trying not to make it noticeable he was looking at him, but doing a terrible job of it. Henry guessed that a German onboard a primarily English ship would raise some eyebrows, but the war was over wasn't it? Certainly, after many years, prejudices would have stopped? Henry strode farther down the side, not wanting to remain in the same spot any longer, and took in the same scenery that he had been seeing for days. His stomach grumbled, as all he could see for miles was open ocean. It was chilly to be sure, worthy of the heavy cloak he had borrowed from one of the friendlier civilians on board, but refreshing all the same. He never realized how much he loved the ocean; the sound of the waves hitting the bow of the large ship, and the salty spray that clung to his cheeks like cold mist, returned vigor to his soul. He felt alive here, mostly because he was on a one-way trip to his destination. There would be no turning back. Nothing could stop him out here.

Henry awoke with a start in the middle of the night, lifting his head, somehow thinking that something was happening. His breathing quickened, but decided he must have been dreaming, but couldn't remember it. He felt wide-awake and decided to head up to the top to get some fresh air. The boat was sailing now in more choppy waters, and Henry had to cling to the railing to keep his footing. Even with almost a week under his belt, his stomach still churned with each rocking of the ship. Long and deep the boat swayed from side to side, lifted up and down from the large waves that stood in its way. A fog had rolled in, as it was still very early in the morning, and with no light from the sun or the moon, every step was taken with precaution. Lights dangled from the ship, but offered only enough light to see a few steps ahead. Deciding that he had enough, which was making him sick, Henry stood by one such light to get his balance, and calm his insides before returning to bed.

It was only a moment later that two figures emerged from the dark, to just inside the light where Henry was standing. They were definitely army personnel, but other than that he couldn't recognize them. "Hello." Henry called out, pretty sure that they weren't out for a midnight stroll purely for pleasure.

No response came, except for one of them showing the other a piece of paper, which then led to both of them looking back at Henry. They nodded to each other, quickly recognizing the accent that they had become so familiar with. They took one step closer, putting them only six feet or so from him, but still making it difficult to see what they were doing. "Hello there," Henry offered again, not liking the situation one bit. With an entire ship to travel, two of them standing so close to him couldn't be good. Henry squinted and washed a spray of salt water from his eyes, finally recognizing one of the men as the same one that had walked past him the day before. He was the one holding the piece of paper and now looking directly at him. Henry noticed the sets of eyes scan his neck, looking at the scar that remained there. After another agonizing minute, the second man took the final few strides to come face to face with Henry.

"Up so early?" he asked sarcastically.

Henry sensed his tone of voice wasn't all together pleasant. "Just trying to get a breath of fresh air," he replied in his best English.

The man leaned back to take one more look at the piece of paper that the first one held up a step behind him, and then turned again to Henry.

"Papers?" the officer asked matter-of-factly.

Henry paused for a second.

"Papers?" Henry tried to sound confused, but took a deep breath ready for what might come next.

"Your traveling papers." The army man wasn't amused. "Do you have them?"

"Not here." Henry's mind raced trying to decide how to answer.

"In your cabin then?"

"Not exactly." Henry's voice quivered.

A gust of fog and mist blew between them, giving him a chill that ran down his spine.

"Where then?" The officer's answers were short and to the point.

"I've lost them. Back at home. In Germany."

Henry knew that the conversation was about to take a turn for the worse.

The uniformed man's hand slid down his side to where Henry presumed his sidearm was kept. He had seen this action before, and it never brought good news.

Henry's pulse quickened as sweat collected on his forehead. He closed his eyes, wondering what was happening, but that made him only look all the more guilty of something he didn't do, or thought he didn't do. The man stood facing him, barely moving an inch, only signaling the first army man over with a nod of his head. Within seconds, handcuffs were tightly gripping the wrists of the German traveler, and he was being led below deck.

"What is the problem, sir?" Henry tried to ask.

"Better for you, if you just keep your mouth shut," was the short reply. "You'll have ample opportunity to talk when the time is right."

Leading them down several decks and to where Henry presumed the engine was, the trio stopped in front of a steel door being held open by a large Englishman.

"This will have to do," the man stated, "haven't had much use for this room in a while now." The man was in civilian clothes and wore a thick blue coat that hung to his knees. His face was unshaven, but looked as one that garnered respect. "Good enough, Captain," the officer answered, as he shoved Henry past him and into the small room. With only a quick pat down for weapons, the door slammed shut and the door's lock engaged. With only a small light swinging from the low roof, Henry's accommodation came slowly into view. "This is definitely no cruise liner," Henry quippedm trying to find some measure of humour in this predicament, but he sat with a thump on what was to be his bed, and didn't.

Ironically enough the bed inside was in better shape than his own, and with absolutely nothing else to do, he lay down and tried to sleep, even though he knew that he wouldn't be able to. He lay on the hard bed staring at the single light, which cast shadows back and forth as the ship swayed, wondering what sort of mess he was in now. For some reason, other than the obvious, he wasn't all that worried. After all, he was finally on his way to Canada, to the province of Nova Scotia. He had traveled to the port on his own, managed to buy a ticket on a ship that sailed that very day. And now he was only days away from delivering his precious cargo. This was his destiny. His journey no one else could have completed. Caressing the envelope from inside his coat, he couldn't see anything or anyone taking him away from his mission. His mission. This must be some mistake. It must be.

It would be many hours before Henry's eyes fell for the last time and he drifted into a restless sleep. The last thing he thought about was his old apartment, the papers that lay inside the rubble, and the bodies that lay beside them. After finally falling asleep, he awoke with a start, only to hear the iron door being unlocked and swinging open with a thud. Shaking away the mental cobwebs, which weren't even fully formed, Henry rubbed his eyes as they adjusted to the new light streaming in from the corridor. "Thank you, Captain," an unfamiliar voice stated. From outside the small cramped cabin, strode a new face. Dressed in military garb he entered casually, not addressing Henry, not even with a glance. Behind him a much larger man walked through the entrance, carrying a small wooden stool, and shut the door with a clunk. With barely enough room to breathe, the uniformed man leaned against the wall opposite the bed and nodded at his companion, who plunked the stool in the centre of the tiny room and backed up to lean himself against the door.

"Please sit down," the man in charge asked politely.

Henry, who didn't see that he had much choice, and hoped that this misunderstanding would soon be over, lifted himself out of bed and sat down wearing only his undergarments.

"Your name, please?" the officer asked.

Henry looked curiously at the man, who certainly seemed cordial enough, "Henry. Dr. Henry Meier."

"Doctor?" the man cocked his head to the side and smiled ever so slightly. "Papers?"

Henry hated that question.

"I'm sorry. My home was destroyed in the war, along with everything I owned."

The uniformed officer glanced over at the large man who still stood silently across the room. The man saw something in his eyes, so he took the one step that brought him behind Henry, who glanced at him nervously.

"Wife? Children? Anyone who can vouch for you?" the officer asked, his cordial politeness wearing thinner.

Henry stared at the man for a second then closed his eyes tightly, letting the memory hit him hard. "They died. They both died in our apartment." Henry bowed his head; hating the fact that he had to remember them, and more than that, remember the state that he had left them in.

The officer seemed to lift Henry's head with his eyes, staring at him in a way that scared him. Henry couldn't break the gaze that held him fast. It was as if he was boring into his skull, deep into his mind, determining if his story was true.

"Is that the story you want to stick to?"

Henry found it impossible to rip his eyes from the man's glare, "I swear, sir. It's true."

The uniformed man held his gaze for a moment longer and then broke it, lifting his eyes to look back at the large man that stood behind the chair. Sweat dripped from Henry's forehead, feeling the intensity of the moment. The room felt as if it was shrinking in size, if that was possible, putting the three of them almost on top of each other. The tiny light bulb offered little light and it swung freely with the rocking of the ship, casting shadows on the military man's face. Henry tried to think of what he could have done to deserve this treatment. Did he wrong someone? He racked his brain thinking of how to get himself out of this predicament.

"There must be someone who can vouch for me, sir, "Henry offered. "A patient, someone at the hospital, someone…"

Henry stopped. The breath in his lungs left him. Instantly pain followed. The man behind him had slammed his fist into the ribs of the unwary suspect. Henry lurched forward, almost dropping to the ground in pain. He opened his mouth wide trying to get air to go in, but none would. His side ached enormously. His heart beat faster and faster, feeling as if his ribs had been smashed like an egg. Henry looked up in pain, thinking of little else than shoving air down his throat. Scanning the eyes of the man across from him, he found no sympathy or regret.

"Hurts, don't it?" was all the response he got.

Chapter Eighteen

It would seem hours, but really would only be a minute, before the precious air finally filtered down into Henry's system. His side ached more and more, but at least he could breathe.

"Now," the officer continued, "this is your last chance before things get taken to the next level. What is your name?"

Henry, still grabbing the side of his chest, wondered desperately what was going on. "I don't understand, sir; my name is Dr. Henry Meier."

Wham. The large man's fist sunk into Henry's side again; the opposite side, this time. Henry's breath left him again, even more quickly than the last time. Funny, but the pain didn't feel as bad this time, partly because he couldn't feel anything. He lurched forward and fell onto the floor, his head turned toward the feet of the officer, who stood in place. Henry's eyes fogged over, his breath still gone, his chest heaving, looking as if he was throwing up. The thought of never breathing again was the last thing he remembered. That and the sight of brightly shined boots pointed inches from his forehead.

"Is she going to be all right?" asked the pastor, standing over her bedside.

"That depends on what your definition is of all right." the nurse commented, changing a dressing on the patient's head.

The concerned pastor stood, compassionately reaching down to hold Lizzy's hand and closing his eyes for a brief moment, saying a prayer. Opening his eyes, he turned to the nurse again hoping for something else, but not sure what to ask for. The nurse didn't offer anything, but continued to pull away the bloodstained bandage wrapped around the circumference of the patient's head. With a less than gentle tug, Lizzy's eyes shut tightly and then she gasped quietly with the pain. The pastor noticed first, and motioned to the nurse, who was already pushing a button beside the bed.

"I saw it, Reverend," the nurse confirmed. "The doctor will be in shortly."

Just as she predicted, one of the doctors rounded the corner and strode into the sterile room, to see what the problem was.

"She is showing signs of feeling pain stimulus, doctor." the attending nurse informed him, holding the loose end of the bandage, but not pulling it any farther.

"Good. Good," the doctor mumbled. "Let me take a look."

Elizabeth's face had returned to its lifeless state, but once the doctor took hold of the bandage and gave it another quick tug, her eyes shot open and winced from the pain.

"Welcome back, Elizabeth," the doctor commented, already placing his stethoscope at her chest and instructing the nurse to take her pulse. The fog lifted very slowly, but the pain in her head certainly helped her regain consciousness. "What…where am I," Lizzy fumbled, trying to lift her hand to her head, but could not. The doctor and nurse continued to take measurements and heartbeats, at first in a hurried state, but now slower and more methodical. The pastor had taken one step back, allowing the hospital staff to do their work. But when it became obvious the patient was stable, he took his step back toward the bed.

"You're in the hospital, Elizabeth." A smile cracked the pastor's face, trying to put on a brave front for the waking patient.

"Hospital," Lizzy struggled to understand. "What happened?"

The doctor interjected, putting away his tools and looking now at his patient directly. "You've had an accident, but you'll be all right soon." Lizzy tried to rub her throbbing head, which throbbed all the more as the nurse finished pulling the bandage off and started to clean the wound, before placing a new one around it.

"Rest now, okay?" the doctor added. "I'll be back in a while to check on you again. Can I speak to you, Reverend?" he said, now turning to face the visitor.

"Of course."

The doctor put a gentle hand on his arm and led him to the back of the room by the door. "Is there anyone I can talk to? Family perhaps?"

"I don't think so, none that I know of. In fact, she hasn't talked to anyone in quite a while." The pastor sighed.

"She will recover from her head and shoulder wound, in time."The doctor paused, "I'm not so sure about her addiction, though."

"Alcohol, you mean."

"Yes," the doctor took a deep breath. "The sweating, tremors, hallucinations; they will still go on for a while until it all gets purged from her system."

"What can I do?" the Pastor asked.

"Just be with her. For now, just be with her."

The doctor reached for the clipboard hanging by the door and flipped over the top page.

"There is a more serious issue, though," the doctor added slowly. "We did find something in the blood work, we had suspected."

He turned to the pastor, lowering the clipboard, gaining his full attention.

"Cirrhosis in the liver."

"Oh my." The pastor gasped.

"We'll do a few more tests to be sure, but it certainly looks that way."

"Will she be all right?"

"It's tough to say. Right now, the best thing for her is to stay away from the booze, and get herself on a strict diet. Long term, though, it will be a wait and see approach."

"Will she die?" the pastor questioned, feeling all the more terrible about the situation Lizzy had placed herself in.

"Realistically?" the doctor waiting for the nodded approval of the pastor to continue, "it will depend on the patient and if her body can repair itself sufficiently…but in some severe cases, it is terminal."

"And in *her* case", the pastor prodded.

"Looks as if she has been drinking heavily for some time. There is a lot of damage there." He turned with a sad look at his patient. "I would pray for her."

The pastor turned to where the doctor's gaze rested, seeing Elizabeth lying in the bed looking around, her mind still in a fog. Her face was gleaming with sweat, and her hair was a mess, notwithstanding the bandages that boldly stood out on her head and on her shoulder. Elizabeth looked desperate. The doctor replaced the clipboard and walked out of the room, followed shortly after by the nurse who had finished all of the necessary tests.

The pastor had his own life to lead. He had his own congregation to serve. He had a family and friends to be in fellowship with, but this was important too. He couldn't abandon her, as she believed everyone else had. He would stand the test of time, until God decided otherwise. Gently walking to her bedside, he placed his hand on hers.

"Why can't I lift my hands and legs?" Lizzy asked groggily.

The pastor touched the straps that held her down, not allowing her to move freely, and then touched a small scar that remained hidden under his collar. "A couple of days ago, you woke up screaming." The pastor rubbed the small wound for a brief moment then re-adjusted his collar.

"You got violent." He smiled as best as he could for her, but secretly wanted to cry.

Lizzy lay in her bed, trying to figure out what was happening to her. She searched deep into her memories of anything that could explain what was going on. All she could bring forward was the bad, the evil things that had happened to her; a home in disarray, her mouth on a half-opened liquor bottle. She remembered her brother was long gone. She knew her husband-to-be was gone. He wouldn't be coming home, even after his promise. Now she was strapped down in a bed, with a tube coming out of her arm, and a poor actor of a reverend pretending that everything was okay.

"I'm in prison," Lizzy mumbled silently. "I'm in prison, on death row."

To say that Henry woke in the middle of the night would be correct if only he had really slept any form of proper sleep, the sleep where you feel more rested when you awoke. It was the intense pain in Henry's ribs that shook him from the darkness of unconsciousness. He was glad to feel that he was at least breathing, and reached down to feel a large bandage wrapped around the circumference of his chest. Just the slightest touch of his hand on his side made him wince. He might have broken a few ribs, he figured, or at least cracked them very badly. The tiny single light above him still offered a small measure of light, revealing to him someone had indeed come down after he had passed out, and crudely bandaged his chest. He would need more medical attention, to be sure, but he doubted that would come any time soon. He wondered how long he was out for, but his stomach told him quite a while.

He was happy, and a little surprised, then, to see a small tray of food left for him just inside the door on the floor. By some cruel joke, the plate held food that would have been bad enough warm, but now was cold as ice, and in any other circumstance would have been fit for garbage, but Henry dug into it hoping that the faster he ate it, the less he would have to smell it. His stomach somewhat satisfied, Henry shoved the empty tray under the door into the empty hallway, and gently rolled himself back into bed. His every move brought excruciating pain, but after a curse or two, he got as comfortable as he was going to get. With no way of turning the light off, he stared at the shadows dancing back and forth, and waited for the eventuality of sleep.

This must be a mistake, Henry thought, doubt creeping in with every breath. Maybe he wronged someone, or misdiagnosed a patient during the war. But did he deserve to be tortured for that? What did he do that deserved this kind of treatment? After all he had done for the English, the lives that he had saved. Could he be that bad a person? And why did they doubt his identity so? Could they not believe who he is? Why the questions? Why the fists? Henry slammed his own fist into the cement wall beside his bed, with a low thud, sending a jab of pain from his side, telling him to stop that. He cursed some more, feeling as if God himself was trying to stop him from what good he was trying to do.

"What is your problem?" Henry called out. "Can't you leave me alone?"

Henry slammed his fist into the wall again, sending another surge of pain from his ribs, making him all the more angry.

"Damn you!" Henry yelled.

It was all he could do, until he finally fell asleep, his body forcing him to rest, as uncomfortable as it was.

It would be far into the morning before Henry woke up again. This time, the pain felt slightly less intense but it still gave him more than enough discomfort with every movement. His body was beginning to go numb with the pain, almost as if his mind was trying its best to give Henry some reprieve from the actual pain, by not letting his body feel it. As a Freudian dog would do, he scanned the door hoping to find a tray of food, no matter what shape it took, but saw none. Wincing with the pain he still felt, which was still significant, he looked up to see the small light still shining, but for the first time in days, hanging at rest. Henry struggled to climb to a sitting position, and with nothing else to do, rubbed his sides gently while waiting for something to happen.

It was an hour or so later when the ship's horn blasted, disturbing the silence. Within minutes the boat shook slightly, as if it had hit someone gently. It certainly felt as if they had docked. Another hour or so passed before the small iron door unlatched and opened. Henry instinctively moved to the far side of the bed, wondering what sort of punishment was in store for him this time. Grabbing his bandaged sides, he grimaced as he shuffled along the side of the bed, waiting for someone to enter the room.

"Good morning," the officer exclaimed as he entered the small room. It was the same officer that had talked to him some nights ago on the top deck. His voice had little joy in it. The man stood at the door impatiently, apparently waiting for something. "Well, let's go." Henry stared back, unsure of what to do. "We're here. And you're going." The uniformed man smiled ever so briefly.

With almost too much pain to handle, Henry was escorted by the lone officer up the flights of stairs and along the main deck where a military vehicle was waiting for him. Henry hobbled along, bracing himself against the off-white iron walls that extended the length of the deck. No one offered any sympathies or help, and after every few steps, Henry tried to slow down and stop to catch his breath, but was only given a stern command to keep going. Henry finally crossed the pedestrian boarding plank that stretched out from the ship onto the busy dock. Looking down the length of the ship, Henry caught sight of another crossing farther down, where the other personnel were disembarking.

"What's going to happen to me?" Henry questioned the man walking behind him.

No answer came immediately, but once he had climbed into the empty rear compartment of the awaiting vehicle, with the door about to slam shut, the officer finally responded.

"Nothing I would be looking forward to." The man smirked, turning to Henry with another small grin on his face before returning to his other duties.

Most of the daylight was extinguished as the double rear doors slammed on him, with only a small fraction of light coming from two tiny windows on either side of the compartment. Both were protected with an iron bar welded firmly through the middle. *"As if they were big enough to slide through anyway,"* Henry thought sarcastically. One unpadded iron bench lined each side of the compartment. Room enough to cram a few prisoners, but he was the only occupant. No seat belts or handles to offer stability, giving Henry the uncomfortable duty of having to reach across the length of the vehicle to brace himself, as the vehicle lurched forward.

Henry's sides ached terribly as the paddy wagon bounced along the road. Sunlight streamed in when the vehicle faced the proper direction, allowing Henry a brief but welcomed warmth to his face. Every bump in the road shot pain up the doctor's sides and into his head, giving him a terrible headache. It was an hour's drive, on mostly city streets, before the road that the vehicle traveled on turned for the worse. The green and black army vehicle turned off the paved road and onto a dirt road leading out of the city. Henry strained to look out of the small window, to find only trees. Every couple of seconds the vehicle bounced hard, as it ran over potholes and small ditches, giving Henry fits of pain. It was as if the two drivers steered deliberately into them, causing Henry to vault up and down with every one. The prisoner's head slammed into the rear doors as the vehicle slowed to dive into a small ditch, and as the engine roared, it climbed the embankment, sending it skyward. Drops of blood fell from his face as he slid back and forth. His head screamed with pain, and his ribs were on fire, with no signs of getting to their destination. He hadn't felt this type of pain before and once again, Henry's frail body couldn't take it. Falling to the floor, feet facing the rear doors, Henry passed out, leaving his body to the whims of the driver.

Chapter Nineteen

THE VEHICLE TRAVELLED for another half hour or so, before finally coming to a stop. Blood dripped from various places along Henry's body, as it lay limp on the vehicle floor.

Like an old warped record player skipping the same tune, Henry awoke to find himself both in a jail cell and in immeasurable pain. He lifted his head high enough to only see brick and mortar for walls and an iron-barred door blocking passage to the outside world. His room was much larger than the one in the ship, and he did notice a table and two chairs in the centre of his room. The pain from the day before caught up to him in a heartbeat and he slid his free hand up and down his body to touch the most painful spots, which were numerous. Bandages lined his head, chest and leg. As only a doctor would, he felt the bandages, feeling a more professional effort was put into placing them, but the intense pain offered him no relief from thinking of much else. His head swam as he tried to lift it further to see beyond the bars that held him. He let his head fall onto the pillow provided, and he closed his eyes to let sleep wash over him once again.

It would be hours before the unwilling prisoner would wake again. This time it was the loud clanking of the iron bars that made him stir.

"Someone here to see you." a voice called out from beyond the steel door. Henry stirred restlessly, opening and closing his eyes frequently, trying to brush the cobwebs out. With only a brief repositioning of his body, in order to turn to the voice, he was reminded of the limitations his body was placing on him.

He was unable to respond quickly enough to question the voice's comment before the steel-bar door clunked as it was unlocked and opened to let in his first visitor. In walked a small man, who Henry would learn eventually to be a public servant, dressed in a simple dark suit, and dark-rimmed glasses. Without asking for permission or advice, the man plunked his briefcase down on the table and sat down on one of the chairs provided. "My, my." the man stated, without much emotion, as he shook his head in pity looking at Henry lying in the cot. Henry had adjusted himself ever so slightly so as to see the visitor, but still was at a loss to ask any questions. "They did say you fell out of the truck, but I didn't realize that you were in such bad a shape." Lying on the bed, the prisoner furrowed his eyes. Sensing the displeasure on his client's face, the man shook his head again and returned to his briefcase, opening the buckle that held it shut. "I didn't believe that story, either," the small man admitted. "Now. I only have a few minutes here, so I need to ask you a few questions."

With much pain, Henry lifted his one arm to raise his head up off the bed, uncertain still as to what was going on, but believing that he might receive some answers from the person in his cell.

"Who are you?" was all he could muster to start.

"I am your lawyer, "the man responded, reaching out to shake his client's hand but retracting it quickly realizing that it most likely wouldn't be accepted. "Mr. Burrows is my name. I have been appointed as your defendant in this matter."

"What matter?" Henry probed.

"Well," the lawyer took a deep breath. "Let me ask you first your name."

"Dr. Henry Meier. I have told that to enough people already."

"I know, but I wanted to hear it for myself." The lawyer flipped through a few pages of briefs then placed it back on the table. "Am I correct in assuming that you have no papers or identification?"

Henry's face grew redder than a ripe tomato, "Of course not, no! How many times must I say that I do not? They were all destroyed in the war."

"I'm sorry sir, but you have to understand that I must ask you this for my own benefit."

The lawyer reached into his briefcase again and pulled out a small pad of paper and a pen and began to jot down some notes. Growing ever more impatient, the broken prisoner pushed himself as far up on his elbow as he could to look at what his newfound lawyer was doing,

"Can you get me out of here? I have an important…"

Henry stopped mid-sentence. His mouth dropped with the realization that he hadn't remembered the letter since the fateful night on the top deck of the ocean ship. He couldn't believe that he hadn't remembered it before, but with the stress of being put under arrest, not to mention the constant beatings, it was no wonder.

"No excuse," Henry mumbled as he ran his hands down the length of his body searching with little hope that the letter would still be tucked into one of his pockets. In fact, he hadn't remembered missing his entire suitcase or his coat, in the events of the past days. None of that was important, however, compared to the precious cargo he had kept in his coat pocket. "No excuse," he repeated over and over, as a madman would, searching each fold of his clothing.

Looking up from his pad, the lawyer saw the new and explosive emotion coming from his client.

"What's the matter?"

"My letter," Henry panted desperately, "my letter is gone. They've taken it away from me. How could they do that? I need it. I need it."

With each breath Henry grew more desperate. Sweat crested his forehead and his head collapsed back onto his pillow, falling from his hand, which couldn't hold it anymore.

"What letter?" Mr. Burrows asked.

"My letter. My letter," was all that Henry was able to muster breathing the words over and over.

Whack. Whack.

One of the prison wardens rapped hard on the steel doors, causing Mr. Burrows to swing around suddenly.

"Time's up, lawyer!" the guard announced.

Mr. Burrows gathered up his papers and stuffed them all back into his briefcase and pushed himself up from the table. He leaned over to Henry who stared blankly at the sky still muttering the words over and over.

"I won't be back for a while, I'm afraid. I'm only here as a courtesy as it is. There must be some record of you somewhere in Germany, but with the war and everything I'm not sure if I'll find anything. I'll do my best, and get back to you as soon as I can."

The lawyer walked toward the open steel door and turned one last time to Henry lying in a state of pity. "I'll look into this *letter* for you as well." With that, he turned to walk out of the cell. The barred door slammed shut with authority, leaving Henry to mutter to himself, as a madman would, sliding deeper into insanity.

Henry's mind drew a blank as he muttered about his letter. The pain in his side and head were as intense as before, but Henry didn't acknowledge them. He shook his head in disbelief. All he could do was fear that his life was over. It didn't matter anymore how much his body burned. It didn't matter what the English would do to him. If he couldn't complete his mission it would mean nothing. He would be nothing.

Henry drifted in and out of reality. He saw himself lying in the bed, dressed up in blood-stained bandages. His mind took him across the ocean to his home country, standing beside the body of an English soldier. He looked into the dead hollow eyes of the soldier who gave him, and only to him, his final request. He saw the face of Elizabeth looking back at him in anger. She turned from him in disgust. He finally saw the eyes of Carmen looking into his. He saw the fear and terror as tonnes of rock and ash fell on top of her. Just before her body collapsed in the rubble his mind went blank, as he slipped into unconsciousness.

It was the smell of a hot plate of food that finally woke him up from a restless but deep sleep. Henry opened his eyes ever so gently, letting the light filter in slowly. At first, he couldn't remember where he was and why, but that changed seeing the brick and mortar staring back at him. It was only an instant later that he remembered his predicament—not the one of being trapped inside a foreign jail accused of something he didn't do, but of letting the letter fall out of his hands and away from its destination.

He closed his eyes again in heart-wrenching sorrow. He held his eyes tight for a long time, not wanting to face reality. He had always thought himself a strong person; someone of character and of commitment, but this was too much for him to handle. His life was, for all intents and purposes, over. He had no reason to live anymore. God had seen to that. He had taken everything from him. Even what he sought to do on his own, God took away. He would cry, but would still not give Him the satisfaction.

He let his mind go on cruise control, desiring not to think about anything beyond the four walls that kept him confined. Inside he desperately wanted to know where his letter was, but the pain of knowing it was lost forever hurt too much. Lying still with his head on the pillow, Henry noticed the pain in his head and side had subsided somewhat, but as soon as he moved to see where the aroma was coming from, it came back. It wasn't as intense as before but it was still more than a little uncomfortable. Taking his time to lift his head up off the pillow, he looked down to see a plate full of food that couldn't have been placed there more than a few minutes ago. Beside it lay a plain glass filled with water. The food certainly smelled good, at least to him in his condition. It might have been the *other* pain in his stomach or his cracked and parched lips, but the contents on the tray set before him seemed fit for a king. Unfortunately, as much as the prisoner wanted to dig in and scarf it down, he would have to sit up first. Henry took more than a few minutes just to lift himself up into a sitting position on the bed. The pain would be tolerated, balanced by the need for some sustenance. Once he finally lifted the tray up to his knees and got the first mouthful inside him, he felt measurably better. Each mouthful went down quicker than the one before, and the glass of luke-warm water washed each one down until every last crumb was gone.

By the time he was finished, which wasn't very long, Henry's spirits rose ever so slightly. For the first time in as long as he could remember, his stomach wasn't rumbling.

Henry rested the empty tray on his lap and tilted the glass up high to suck the last few drops of water, as the iron door of his cell unlocked to find another army man standing there. "I hope you enjoyed your meal?" he asked plainly. Henry looked at the officer who wore his green and grey camouflage fatigues. He wore more than a few medals that dangled from his left chest pocket. He didn't recognize this particular uniform right away, as it wasn't one of the ones that he had seen lately. Most of the personnel here and on the boat he had traveled on, had worn a more formal military wear. Henry had neither the desire nor the willpower to smile or to reply. "Maybe you can repay me the favour and answer a few questions?" the decorated officer probed. Henry turned back to the empty tray in front of him and stared at it silently. The officer moved into the lone occupant's cell and gently pushed the table and chairs together, as if ready to do some spring-cleaning.

"My name is Captain Carver. I have been assigned to interrogate you."

Henry glanced up at the middle-aged man, noticing the politeness in his voice. The officer leaned gently on one side of the table and stared at Henry, who looked more than uncomfortable sitting on the bed with the tray still on his knees and the empty glass in one hand. The interrogator reached over and took the tray and glass from Henry and placed it on the table behind him. "I know you have had a difficult time so far, so may I ask you a simple question then?"

Henry continued to stare at his visitor, as if caught in a trance. "What is your name?" the man asked.

Chapter Twenty

Henry took a deep breath, "my name is Dr. Henry Meier." Henry said it plainly and quietly. He almost felt as if he should have answered it a different way, but it was the truth, it had always been the truth. And no matter the consequence, it didn't matter now anyway. "You may have figured out by now, that is not the answer I was looking for." Henry continued to stare at the man with little care. His interrogator continued, "I've been invited here to confirm your identity." He paused for a few seconds. "We know who you are. And the United States Army will make sure you receive the punishment you deserve." Henry's eyes widened, feeling more nervous than he would admit to. Sitting on the bed for so long started to induce pain in his ribs and side, making him list to one side in an effort to ease the strain on his ravaged body.

"Now, I can see you're not in the best shape of your life, but my advice to you would be to admit who you are and to what you have done and we can end this little charade." Henry could tell that Captain Carver was from the U.S. army. His accent was certainly different from the Canadians he had encountered. He felt uneasy about the man standing in front of him. Henry thought of himself as a good judge of character, but this one he couldn't figure out. He talked as if he wanted to be friends, but deep in his voice, there was an anger that scared him. It was clear that this was an officer who was used to getting what he wanted, and had the ego and the temperament to speak in tones that demanded it. If his own situation weren't so desperate, he would be more inclined to fear what this man was capable of. "My letter is gone," Henry thought, staring into the army man's eyes. He has taken my very soul away.

Captain Carver lifted himself up from the table, and took two steps to plunk himself down beside Henry on the bed. Even with the bed as hard as it was, just the motion of another person sitting down beside him shot pain through his chest.

"I have given you the courtesy of counsel, and I will allow you to heal before we talk again. But I hope you decide to start telling the truth." Henry felt a hand being placed gently over top of his bandages along his chest. The hand began to push into his side slowly but solidly. The pain was terrible. "You don't want our relationship to continue for an extended period of time." Just as quickly as the pressure was applied, it was removed, leaving Henry to wince on the bed. The interrogator lifted himself off the bed and walked to the open door, stopping but not turning around. "I will break you, you know." he told Henry as he stood there. The pain in Henry's side stirred up the anger that welled up inside him. His world had collapsed and his life had been taken from him. He had nothing left to give and nothing more to answer for. Pain was all that he had left. "I'm already broken." Henry responded as defiantly as he could.

The uniformed man in the doorway stood in place for a moment longer, then continued down the hallway out of sight. Henry watched him go, not sure what he felt or what he should feel. A younger Canadian soldier emerged from the shadow beyond the door, to shut the steel door tight and lock it. Henry sat on the bed, staring out into nothingness. He was nothing now. He couldn't feel happy or sad. He couldn't remember being loved or finding joy in the simple things he did. All that was real inside him was gone, and only a broken body was left to endure what more pain lied ahead. It didn't matter. Pain was all he had to remind him that he still breathed. As gently as he could, he shuffled to put his head back on the pillow and stared up at the bricks that lined the ceiling.

He wasn't as tired as he had hoped, wanting to drift back to sleep, hoping this nightmare would be over and he would wake up to a different life and in a different place.

Henry stared for hours, having neither the willpower nor the resources to do anything else. Henry tried to look up to the red and black ceiling and to think of nothing, but he couldn't. His mind raced from event to event that led him to his current situation. Over and over he contemplated what he should have done differently, or what he might have done wrong. He didn't see any flaws in his plans, he only saw a God that wished him not to succeed. Thinking of it over and over just made him madder, until he could hardly stand it. Finally, he decided to focus on three things that would keep him occupied. First, that he hated the English Army, and the betrayal that he felt. Second, that he would learn to hate Captain Carver and what he was trying to do, and especially how he would do it, and that he wouldn't give him the satisfaction of whatever he was seeking. But mostly that he hated God. Hated Him for all that he had done to him.

Hours later, Henry closed his eyes for the final time and drifted into a sleep that while still uncomfortable, was satisfying.

It was the unlocking of the iron-barred door again that aroused the prisoner from his sleep. Henry took a deep breath, feeling better with a good night's sleep. He dared not move though, feeling no need to, and not wanting to test the limits of his injuries. "Good morning, sir." a voice called out from beside the bed. Henry tilted his head to see a short black-haired man, who obviously had coloured his hair to hide an increasing amount of grey. He wore a very familiar white lab coat and carried an even more familiar brown leather case in one hand. Henry hadn't the desire to answer back, but was interested at least to see what new turn of events were happening.

"I'm Doctor Chase," the man answered without being asked. "I've been assigned to help you get better, though I'm afraid for what purpose." The doctor shook his head thinking of a previous conversation that he had had with Captain Carver, and pulled one of the chairs closer to the bed in order to sit next to his new patient. Henry continued to stare at the doctor as he put down his medical bag and stared back at him. "I don't know what to believe, but apparently they don't have the proper personnel here to take care of you, so I've come from the local hospital to take care of you as best as I can from inside this un-sterile cell."

Henry cracked a small smile, as he felt an instant kinship to the man across from him. He could somehow see a different place or a different time, where he might be sitting on the chair and another person was lying in the bed across from him. He would have the same doubts and the same worries but would tend the patient as best as he could. "My name is Dr. Henry Meier." Henry told him, wanting the other man to reciprocate his own feelings. Unfortunately, his colleague didn't respond, but merely smiled as you would to someone you felt incredibly sorry for. With a deep breath, Dr. Chase removed a small pad of paper and pencil and looked at Henry with a hint of hesitation. "Can you tell me where it hurts?"

The question seemed somewhat humorous to Henry who lay in bed with bandages wrapped up along his body. But a question he would have asked, if also given little information of a patient's injuries. "Starting at the top," Henry started. "I've sustained more than one concussion, and if nothing else it's giving me one heck of a headache. I don't believe I've suffered any skull fractures, but you'll have to find that out for yourself. It seems I've broken at least one or two ribs, probably one of my false ribs. But due to my wonderfully luxurious cab ride here, I believe I also have developed costochondritis." Henry stopped for a second as the doctor was obviously caught off guard with the more elaborate explanation of injuries, and was quickly jotting down notes.

"I've sustained numerous cuts and wounds to my lower torso, some of them deep, but whoever patched me up the last time did a decent enough job and I don't think they will lead to anything serious. I do worry that with as much trauma as I have received I might end up getting osteomyelitis somewhere, probably in my upper femur. Antibiotics would be a good start, to make sure that doesn't happen." Henry finished his self-diagnosis to the astonishment of the attending physician. Dr. Chase looked back at Henry with a more understanding look. "Your English is quite good," the doctor commented as he finished jotting down notes on his pad of paper. "And your diagnosis is even more thorough. Dr. Henry Meier?" the English doctor asked again rhetorically. "Dr. Henry Meier." Henry said again, thinking that for once in a long while, someone actually believed him.

Taking a few minutes to look over the bandages and take Henry's temperature, Dr. Chase seemed satisfied for the moment. "I'll be back later today or tomorrow with some supplies." Dr. Chase rose from his seat and shoved his tools back into his case. He leaned over and touched Henry gently on the shoulder. "Dr. Henry Meier," he said thoughtfully. "You know, I was led to believe you were someone else." The bandaged patient looked unsurprised. "I'm sorry for what I think they may try to do to you." The doctor took a breath and sighed. He wasn't too naive to know that he was only here to keep Henry from getting worse, or even dying. He wasn't here to rescue him, or to be a counselor. He was here to heal his wounds and make sure he survived whatever they had in mind for him, probably in order to extract what information they desired. But the war was over wasn't it? Dr. Chase couldn't understand why it mattered so much, who or what this man was. The war was over, but, he guessed, not forgotten. Taking another breath, he nodded one more time at his jail-cell patient, "Don't worry, I'll take care of you."

Henry smiled, watching his doctor leave the cell. He felt altogether better. Not that this changed his situation much, but at least someone out there believed him. For the time being Henry's spirit lifted. He even forgot to think about the pain for the moment, as maybe that wasn't the only reminder he needed to confirm that he was alive.

Lizzy opened her eyes to see a familiar face staring back at her. "Good morning, Elizabeth," her pastor smiled gently. Elizabeth rubbed some of the sleep out of her eyes, slowly letting the world back in. She smiled brightly, seeing her pastor and friend next to her. The last few weeks had been hard on her. The first few days she barely remembered. Nightmares of ghosts and demons haunted her. She remembered trying to bat them away, but their hands held her arms down fast, making her wrists burn with pain. She had been given numerous tests, some of which were extremely painful. She had been subjected to more needles and exams than she had had in her entire life. The doctors wanted to be sure they had diagnosed her injuries correctly, and that proper treatment was being undertaken. Through it all, her wonderful pastor had been there. In fact, he had been the only one there. He did tell her that at one time, her old friend had stopped by, but Lizzy didn't remember such a visit. She couldn't understand at first why he had taken so much time out of his life to be with her. He must have had more important things to do, more needy people to see. Didn't he have a family? Friends?

"Good morning." Lizzy smiled again. "Is everything all right?"

The two of them had grown close in the last few weeks, and she could sense something in his eyes. She had known him to be an honest and caring man, not one to hold things back or to sugarcoat the truth. She loved that about him. "Of course," he replied. "Your surgery went well. In fact, they say you can be released in a couple of days, as soon as they finish a couple of final tests." Lizzy could sense something else in his eyes, but wasn't sure what it was.

"I know I've never pushed you about this, but could I pray for you?" The reverend knew how much she had despised God recently, and what she thought He had done to her. He knew that it was more important for him to be at her bedside than to quote scripture, but he felt the urge to do something more, now that her time in the hospital was almost done. Certainly, he had prayed for her many times. In fact, he had spent countless hours praying over her body as it lay on the bed unconscious after a fit of violence brought on by hallucinations. But this time he wanted to pray *with* her.

Elizabeth took her time looking into his eyes before responding. It was true that he had never pushed God on her, even during her most desperate time. He was right to do so, she knew she would have lashed out even more and demanded he leave her alone. But his caring spirit and gentle heart had won her over, and she could now see that deep inside him, it was God that had made him who he was. Her eyes began to well up. She had hated God so badly. Blaming Him for everything that had happened. But looking across the bed, she could see the love He had for her, expressing itself through this man. "Sure," was all that she could say.

The pastor leaned into her, placing his hands over top of hers, which had been released from the straps on the bed some time ago. He gently placed his fingers on the scars that still clung to her wrists, and bowed his head. He prayed a simple yet loving prayer that later on Elizabeth would admit she didn't even remember. All she could do was let the tears flow freely from her eyes. He had won her back, she admitted to herself. As the reverend finished and lifted himself back to his seat beside the bed, Lizzy saw duplicate tears flowing from his eyes as well. "I talked to the doctor before you woke up," he said; the tears didn't stop as he spoke. "I'm afraid that you will never be quite the same." He stopped, unsure of how to explain to her the news he dreaded telling her. Elizabeth could sense the frustration in his voice. "Whatever it is, don't worry. I feel better than I have in many years." "Your liver is beyond repair, and they don't know how long you will live. It may be months or years." The reverend sniffed, trying to hold back the tears that flooded his face. "There is a chance of a transplant, but they don't think it will happen." Elizabeth could sense the empathy in his voice and on his face. She reached over this time, to place her hands on his. "My body may be dying, and I deserve that. But better than any doctor, it is you that has healed me."

"I'm afraid there is something else, though." This time Lizzy's pastor turned slightly, so as to avoid eye contact. Elizabeth could feel the battle in his voice, sensing that a decision was being made, or one had already been made, but one he was not so entirely happy about. "You know that I have grown close to you. Closer even than those that I serve in my congregation." He paused enough to turn back to look into her eyes, Lizzy catching the sadness in them. "I've been called away from here. I don't know why, but I know I must. I am heading to Boston to head up a new church there."

The sudden news hit her hard. It was her turn to look away from the eyes of her pastor. She closed her eyes tightly and tried to figure out why he would leave her, especially now, just as she had seemed to turn a corner. Somehow in her heart, she knew why. He was the most honest and true person that she had ever met. There was no denying he cared for her, and had taken care of her, even when no other would. If he really felt that he had to go, then she would have to accept it. She wouldn't have to like it, though.

"When?" was all that she could ask.

"Tomorrow." The straightforward answer somehow told her that this decision had not come lightly, or all that long ago.

After a time of silence, it was Lizzy who had been healing in both body and spirit, who leaned over to once again embrace her friend.

"I will miss you."

The two of them hugged for a long time and didn't let any more words get in the way. Finally, before he had to leave for the day, and the rest of her life, he offered one last thing.

"I know, deep in my heart, that you will find whatever it is you are looking for. You just have to ask for it."

Lizzy smiled and cried, watching him leave for the final time. She felt confused. She felt a renewed vigor, and a willingness to get better. But why now? Why would he have to leave her now?

Chapter Twenty-One

THE NEXT FEW weeks were the longest of his life. Lying in bed with neither the will, nor ability to move, gave Henry little lust for life. His doctor visited him almost daily, giving him numerous pills and antibiotics to swallow. Changing his bandages and taking tests and measurements were also a daily task. The pulling of blood-soaked and crusty bandages from raw flesh seemed to bring him closer to death each time. There was little banter between the two doctors, partly due to the personalities of each of them, and partly due to the fact that often a young soldier would escort him in and wait patiently until he left. It seemed some of the tools of the trade were not ones that would be tolerated being *forgotten* inside the cell.

After a time, Henry was able to sit up with less discomfort, and eventually even sit himself down at his small table and eat the food provided. It was a change for him to have three regular meals brought to him each day. Using the small toilet was not something he looked forward to, but that would have to be a necessary by-product of eating a healthier diet. His body gained strength with each day, until finally came the time for the doctor to stop coming. Henry sat on the bed, letting Dr. Chase take his temperature again, even though he knew what the results would be. He removed the last of the bandages from Henry's head and legs, revealing the scars that would be a lasting reminder of the torture that he had so far endured. "I'm afraid this is the last time I will have to come see you, my friend." Dr. Chase said, placing the old bandages and medicine into a large sack provided. "You are doing much better and I'm told the local medic can finish up administering your antibiotics." "Thank you." It was all that Henry could say. He didn't mean it in a rude or short way, just that he was grateful for the quality of care that he had been given. Henry glanced beyond the iron bars, expecting to see a certain someone come crashing through, wringing their hands with joy that he was now ripe for more torture. Dr. Chase sensed Henry's discomfort that their time was at an end. He hadn't seen or heard from the captain since he first arrived. It seemed understood that his job was to put the prisoner's body back together until such a time as he could continue his interrogation. "I'm afraid you'll be receiving a visit from the Captain once I've left." He meant it not as a matter of fact, but genuinely hoping it would not be true, but knew it to be. "Doesn't matter," Henry replied. "There isn't any more he can take away from me, that he hasn't already."

Dr. Chase felt sad at what was happening, but couldn't do anything about it. He couldn't even protest to anyone, as he was merely led in and out each day by a young corporal and not seen or heard by anyone else. He guessed that was by design, not giving him any reason to prolong the healing process. With nothing else to say, he gathered the rest of his things and walked out of the cell for the last time. He wasn't leaving a friend or even a colleague, although he had grown to appreciate the extent of Dr. Meier's knowledge. But he still felt sad inside, and would also wonder what would happen to him next. It would only be a matter of hours before Henry's interrogator strode through the ironed-barred doors again.

He was just finishing up his early dinner when Captain Carver walked in, striding in the same manner as he had left, confident in what he was about to do. Behind him walked another man, whose job Henry immediately recognized. He was a large man, dressed in green and black pants with only a tight white undershirt on, which revealed more than a few muscles. The prisoner almost laughed. He had seen this dog-and-pony show before, and while he knew they were serious, something inside him didn't care. It didn't matter what manner of punishment they doled out. They had taken everything they could and left him with nothing. What was the worst they could do? Inflict more pain on him? It was not as if he wasn't used to it by now.

Carver noticed the hint of comedy on his prisoner's face and pounced on it.

"Something funny?"

Carver grabbed the empty tray from the table and threw it out the open door, letting it crash and tumble down the hallway, spraying applesauce bits along the floor and walls. Henry merely sat in his chair. Deep down he was somewhat afraid of what this man would do, but he didn't really care. Carver motioned to the man behind him, and he strode forward, pulling Henry's table from out in front of him in one motion, leaving him sitting all alone in the middle of the room.

"I hear you're all healed up, Doctor?" Captain Carver asked him sarcastically. "Now I'm going to ask you politely one final time, what is your name?" Henry never knew how to properly interrogate someone. Even with his limited service in the war, had never known or seen someone being interrogated. He didn't know that the best way was to wear the prisoner down with one or two simple questions, asking them over and over until the prisoner had no other choice but to answer it in a way that pleased the interrogator. Unfortunately, Henry had no other answer to give. But he was beginning to feel that even if he did, he wouldn't anyway. "Dr. Henry Meier," was his answer, although that would be the last time he was to answer so boldly.

The rest of the evening was something Henry wished he could forget. Slap after slap, punch after punch, the large man struck him with his fists. Not enough to re-injure him to the point of calling a doctor back, but enough to add more bruises and pain to his already fragile body. Over and over he was asked what his name was, but Henry was defiant, even to the point of passing out again. Captain

Carver didn't show any signs of frustration or anger, only repeating the question time and time again, waiting for the right answer to come forward. Finally, the evening was concluded with the prisoner lying down on his bed in pain, wishing for a better life that he knew would never come.

The next day saw no food or water brought to him; even his medication never came. Henry wasted the day wondering if the interrogation was ended or if it had really just begun. As soon as he had fallen asleep, his stomach turning and his lips cracking, the captain barged in again, with his sidekick in tow. The session would start again with more punishment and the same questions. After a few hours they left again, leaving him with a small stale piece of bread and a half-cup of warm water. This went on for days, giving Henry the distinct sensation of what it would feel like to be a punching bag. The questions kept coming, time after time, but Henry blocked them out, expecting and accepting each punch to come with each withheld response. All along, Captain Carver never wavered in his questions or the tone of voice in which he asked them. It would be a week before the frustration wore at him ever so slightly and he tried another tactic that hopefully would draw some response.

Henry sat on the plain aluminum chair as usual, slumped over from the repeated blows, a trickle of blood dripping from his nose. Fresh bruising left a large blue and black ring around his left eye. It was hard for him to focus. Images of a fist hurtling toward his eyes was still held captive in his memory. He wished that this would all be over, hoping for release, but even more hoping for death. "I noticed you arrived with a letter?" Captain Carver exclaimed after a longer than usual pause in the action.

Henry's ears pricked up instantly, and he looked up to see Carver through the sweat that beaded into his eyes. His heart lurched forward, never forgetting the letter that had been lost. He hadn't expected another line of questioning from this brute, especially involving his prize possession, and it threw him off-guard,

Letter to Elizabeth

to say the least. "It is very touching, but somehow I don't think you wrote it," Carver continued gracefully. "I wonder how you got it." Henry didn't know what to say. He had been led to believe it was gone or destroyed. He didn't really think that this brutish man would actually give it back to him, did he? "Where is it?" was all that Henry could ask, feeling the pain in his chest as he talked. "Somewhere close, "Carver smiled. "I bet you would like to have it back?" Henry took deep breaths, his emotions unsure, trying to avoid thinking of the pain still raptured in his body. "What is your name?" continued the captain, hoping now for a proper response.

That was it. Unwavering in his hatred, yet desperate for the letter, he responded emphatically, "Please, tell me who you want me to be and that's who I'll be. Just give me my letter back."

Captain Carver laughed. It made Henry mad. "You'll get your little letter when I say you can; just tell me your name and this will be all over." "But I don't know my name! I don't know my name!" Henry shook as he yelled at the army man standing behind him now. Feeling frustrated didn't even compare to what he was feeling.

For the next several days, Henry was taunted not so much anymore by physical abuse, but with the carrot of the letter. Captain Carver knew that he had struck that nerve he was looking for. Henry screamed at him, begging him to let him have it, asking him to give him a name to acknowledge so that all of this could be over. Henry could feel madness come over him, knowing that the letter would never come, maybe even that it was not really there. The prisoner couldn't stand it any longer, and Captain Carver left him one evening lying on the floor shaking with desperation, his life was truly at an end. He lay on the hard, cold floor feeling lost and alone, more than he had ever had before, as a newborn would do without its mother's comfort. Anger didn't help him anymore; he was broken as far as he could be. Shivering and fading into a fitful sleep, Henry whispered desperately, "God, please." He had passed the breaking point.

The next day came with no visitors. Only a plate of cold food and a glass of water broke the silence of the day. Henry ate it thoughtlessly, his mind unable to focus on anything anymore. Henry eventually got up and as if trained by Pavlov himself, sat on his chair waiting for the iron doors to open up. It was only a repetitive instinct that made him sit on the cool metal chair. He certainly didn't want any more abuse, but was resigned to the fact that it would come, as it always came. Trying not to acknowledge it seemed pointless. He sat in the chair for many hours, his body wavering slightly, not able to balance properly. His one eye was still bruised and bloodied, his sense of balance severely impaired. Henry peered as best as he could through the steel bars, trying to see what was going on outside his little world. He turned his ear to try to hear the footsteps of his nemesis coming down the hallway, as he always did.

Eventually the prisoner gave up. Henry gingerly lifted himself from his chair and plopped himself back down on his bed. His nose twitched as the smell from his bed was nothing like the clean sheets he was used to back home. Even in hard times, Carmen had had the ability to wash their clothes and sheets so that they would miraculously smell like the open countryside. Here, however, his bedspread and even the clothes on his back, were only washed every other week, leaving a smell that reminded him of hospitals rooms after a long and intensive triage session.

His mind was blank, staring up at this ceiling; he didn't even notice when the doors opened to admit a visitor. It was only the tap on the shoulder that made Henry aware of another person. With his senses so dull, he merely turned his head slowly to reveal who was now bothering him, expecting of course, for it to be the illustrious captain.

Henry's eyes widened, surprised not only that it wasn't him, but that it was his lawyer, Mr. Burrows. His larger-than-necessary glasses framed his blue eyes, which exuded joy. His grin from ear to ear confirmed the emotion his eyes were displaying. Almost immediately, Henry sat up gingerly and began to smile himself, although not knowing why, but sensing that something good was about to happen. "Dr. Meier," the lawyer began, trying to sound professional, but having a hard time hiding the great news he was about to reveal. "You're free." Henry looked at him blankly. He couldn't process the information being given to him. Sensing the lack of understanding, Mr. Burrows continued, "You are free, Henry. We've found enough proper documentation to prove who you are." The former prisoner's bottom lip started to quiver. He was free? He was free. "But," Henry started slowly. "But, Captain Carver?" "Don't you worry about him anymore," Mr. Burrows smiled, as if succeeding in beating an opponent at his own game. "He won't be bothering you anymore. In fact, if you wanted to, although I'm not sure how successful we would be, we could sue him for false imprisonment, improper torture techniques, you know, breaking the Geneva Convention and all..."

The lawyer side of Mr. Burrows kicked in as he rambled on about the prospects of taking the United States and Canadian Governments to court. Henry wasn't listening anyhow, and would eventually never have the desire to take action against his captures. He was free. And that was all that mattered right now, as the understanding of it hit him. It was only a few minutes into his lawyer's tirade that Henry realized that now that he was free, he had nowhere to go. He had no reason to leave the jail cell, because he had no mission to accomplish. His brightened face dimmed, as he looked up and sideways thinking of what direction his messed-up life would now go. Sensing the change in Henry's emotion, Mr. Burrows stopped his speech. "Dr. Meier, sorry. I almost forgot." His face was still gleaming, even more now than before, "I have something for you." Henry's breath and heart stopped at once. As if it was being presented on a silver pillow, Mr. Burrows ever so gently pulled out an envelope, and placed it in his lap.

Henry stared down at the familiar colours and dimensions. The name written so profoundly on the front, *Elizabeth*, drew every emotion he had to the forefront. It couldn't be real, could it? "But I thought…" was all that Henry could mutter. "With your citizenship assured, they had no reason to withhold it anymore," his lawyer replied. Henry lowered one hand slowly to touch one edge of the off-white envelope, almost expecting it to disappear as soon as he did. It didn't. Finally taking the envelope in both hands, he opened up the flap and removed the precious letter, still inside. It was almost as if it had never been opened by the captain, he thought, recognizing the folds and creases as if he had written it himself.

Finally, after so long a time, Henry couldn't fight back the emotions that had lodged themselves inside him for so long. At first it was one tear that broke away from his good eye, and then even his swollen eye, that had borne the brunt of abuse, released a teardrop of joy. Looking up into the eyes of his saviour, Henry let go of all that was inside him, crying openly and holding the letter as close to his chest as he could. Mr. Burrows could feel the moment, crying openly as well, breaking the professional look that he was half-heartedly trying to hold. Henry reached over and hugged his lawyer, not caring if he would be hugged back, but he was. The freed prisoner had been given his life back. This time it was nothing that he could have done himself. It was as if God had waited until Henry had been broken so badly, he needed to ask for help, and when he finally did, it was only then that God was able to intervene. Henry cried for his current circumstance, he cried for the pain he had endured in prison. He cried for his wife and child, who long ago had left him. He cried for joy and for pain, for his past, his present and his future. He finally cried for Elizabeth, whom he desperately wanted to find.

Not wanting to spend any more time in the cold, brick-lined prison, Henry gathered up as much strength as he could, and walked out of the cell, head held as high as he could, leaning heavily on his lawyer. Henry shuffled slowly down the hallway that he couldn't remember being led into, and wondered if he would ever see the captain again. Now that he was finally free, the edge of hatred toward him diminished slightly. There was no denying that he would hate him for years to come, but eventually he would understand that he too had a mission to accomplish, and even though he despised the captain's methods, he knew why he had used them. Much evil had come from the latest World War. Many who deserved punishment had escaped from authorities and would never see justice. Henry must have looked like one of them, or at least given them an impression he was one of them. Captain Carver would have to live with his own guilt, having tortured his innocent prisoner so terribly.

Chapter Twenty-Two

Walking through the catacombs that were the military prison installation, Henry felt stronger. Even leaning on Mr. Burrows, he could feel the blood course through his veins, healing him with every step. It was more emotional than physical, of course, but the freed prisoner knew that soon he would be healed of his injuries for good, and gladly away from this prison. Waiting for them outside the front gate, sitting all alone on the dirt floor was Henry's small suitcase, with his doctor's smock draped over it. No one came to apologize, or to offer their assistance now that he was free. He and his lawyer would walk out of the prison, alone and unfettered. Mr. Burrows left Henry to lean against one of the outside fence posts while he picked up his client's things and shoved them into his car.

Leaning on the fence posts that had once imprisoned him, Henry looked up to one of the two towers that lined the front of the military installation. He could make out an officer holding a long weapon watching the gate, and presumably him. Henry could almost sense the disappointment on his face, knowing that he and his army had not succeeded in their misguided attempts to bring him to justice. The freed prisoner rubbed his neck instinctively, thinking of the events that had led him to this place. Gently helping Henry inside the care, his precious lawyer, whom he would probably never see again, drove him to the local hospital to recuperate for a few days, and hopefully find a way to convince him to file action against his captures. Henry knew that would never happen.

Elizabeth sat on her familiar hospital bed looking around, yet not looking anywhere at all. No more tubes stuck out of her arms, no more bandages draped her shoulder or her head. Only scars remained, reminding her of the time she had spent here. There was no one in the room with her, only a small bag packed for her, and a bottle of medicine in her hand, which she would have to take for a long time to come.

Her pastor was gone, leaving her to find a new home and new people to serve. She didn't begrudge him for that, but still missed him desperately. If there was ever a time when she was lonely for companionship, it was now. There was no one she could think of, whom she could call on. No one that would be there for her as her pastor had been. She was healed on the outside, but inside her heart a hole was still left unfilled.

Lizzy wasn't depressed, or on the opposite side, terribly happy. Only longing for someone to come through the door and give her a hug and tell her that everything was going to be all right. She missed her brother, and especially her fiancé. They wouldn't be here for her now, or ever again. She found the will power to lift herself off the bed and walk out of the hospital. One of the nurses patrolling the hallway noticed her and waved goodbye. With some change in her pocket, she thought the most logical thing would be to go home, to start over. She cringed at the thought of entering her forsaken house. She had certainly left it in disarray. She imagined the musty odor, from empty liquor bottles strewn about the house. The yard would be a mess, and the garden in tatters. There was a small hope that maybe someone had taken the time to go there and everything would be crystal clean, but she knew it wouldn't. Her pastor had spent every moment he could with her, and he wouldn't have had time to do anything else. She resigned herself to the fact that cleaning her house would be just, giving her an opportunity to put a tangible element to starting her life over again. It would be more than she could handle, but she would do the best she could. With no one else to help, she would *have* to.

Waiting at the curb near the hospital for her bus to come, she felt the sun that was rising warm her face. She hadn't felt Mother Nature's touch for a long time, and it felt wonderful. Bus service wasn't exactly perfect, so she waited patiently for the metro bus to pick her up. She knew that the ride would take her into the city and then would turn around to head back the way it came. Living out of the city near the coast offered little in the way of transportation. She could take a city cab, but that would cost too much. Better for her to slowly walk home from the bus's last stop, even if that meant hours of hobbling home. Time wasn't an issue anymore. Funny that she was running out of time physically, but there was nothing to rush to anymore, only to live out her days as best as she could.

Riding in the half-empty bus, Elizabeth scanned the scenery around her. Cars sped to and fro, off to wherever they were destined to be. People walked up and down the city streets, each of them oblivious to the other's cares and needs. Everyone had a story to tell, and everyone needed to finish it in their own way. She was one part of a master plan, one that she knew nothing about. There didn't seem any purpose in the path she had walked in life. Why things had happened to her, was a mystery that could never be solved. Was there really someone up there controlling circumstances? Her pastor certainly thought so.

Finally, after what seemed only minutes, the bus lurched to a stop with the bus driver screaming, "Last stop!" Lizzy sat in her seat for a second longer, and then grabbed her small bag, exiting the bus, taking a deep breath. She scanned the area from left to right, not knowing what direction she needed to go, but feeling the need to look around anyway. What struck her was how much things hadn't changed. Somehow, she thought that the world would be a different place when she got out, but in fact little had been altered. She tried to reflect on the master plan that was life. How everyone had a reason for being, and her circumstance was but one of a million others that were being played out in the world. It didn't seem to help her, though.

Standing on the curb, with the bus engine roaring back to life as it made its way back to wherever it was going, Lizzy saw a building that had been hidden by the bus, revealed. It was a church. It wasn't glowing or being lit up by an invisible spotlight. Unseen arms weren't pulling at her to drag her in. It was only a tug in her heart that told her maybe this would in fact be the proper beginning of her new life. She had grown up around churches, and knew what would be inside. That wouldn't be a mystery. Thinking back to her pastor, she felt as if she owed him as much, to at least walk in and in some way thank him for being there for her.

Taking her time to enter the front doors, which stood open, Lizzy let her eyes grow accustomed to the dim lights inside. A sign hanging over the door said *"Welcome"*, yet she could see no one inside. No one greeted her; no person asked her how she was doing. Wandering around, she figured that there would be some sort of welcoming committee waiting to shake hands or give a hug to the strangers that entered, but no one was there. Walking into the sanctuary, Lizzy noticed first the large cross that hung from the ceiling to rest directly in front of the pews. She could hear the organ being played, as quiet as it was, a hymn that sounded strangely familiar, but she couldn't put a name to it.

Not sure of exactly what to do, and with little else to occupy her, Lizzy strode to the front and stared at the large cross hanging in front of her. She peered at it for several minutes, wondering if a beam of light would shine from it and cause her legs to sway, making her kneel in reverence. Nothing happened. She just felt the calm sensation of a place where no one would harm her. Sliding into the first pew, Lizzy continued to stare at the wooden cross, trying to put words to that strange feeling it gave her. There was a presence in the church that she couldn't explain, something that made her feel safe and secure. Lizzy turned to look behind her, expecting now for some reverend or congregation member to stroll up to her and want to pray with her, but none were there. In some weird way, she was disappointed. She remembered a prayer that was said for her in the hospital room, and it had felt good.

She remembered what her pastor had told her, 'you only have to ask.' Now that she was here, Lizzy didn't really know what to ask for. She stretched out to fold her hands, thinking it would be more respectful. The scars on her wrists staring back at her, giving her memories she'd rather not think of, but surely would never forget. She had been damaged to be sure; not only from the fall down the stairs, and the countless trips to the bottle, but ever since the day the two military officers had driven to her door in their black sedan.

Lizzy bowed her head instinctively, and closed her eyes. For several minutes she sat on the hard, wooden pew trying to think of nothing at all. Lost family and friends, a body shaken until broken, crept into her mind relentlessly. Finally, gathering up her thoughts as best she could, she knew what to ask for. "Lord, give me a friend," was all that she said.

Sitting in the vacant church for a long time, with a whisper of organ music in her ear, Lizzy cried.

Ironically, and certainly happily, Henry fell under the care of the only doctor he knew. The same doctor that had cared for him in his jail cell now completed the work that he had started.

Dr. Chase spent extra time in Henry's hospital room trying to learn more about his patient's experiences, that had led them to their first meeting. Now that he was exonerated, Henry's story seemed absolutely amazing. It wasn't often that Dr. Chase was able to converse with a fellow doctor who had lived such an incredible life. Henry didn't think of his story as interesting, only tragic. He had little desire to dredge up all the details of the war, his practice after it had been destroyed, and the boat ride that had brought him here. Henry could sense that Dr. Chase had led a less interesting life here in Canada, and wanted to experience some of the excitement, at least vicariously.

"If he only knew how lucky he was," thought Henry as he tried to steer the conversation back to present times. Dr. Chase felt as if he had been somewhat cheated of an adventurous journey. He had grown up in Nova Scotia, near Gander, but had moved to Toronto to enroll in medical school. Once his term was completed, he was more than happy to accept a junior position in a local hospital in Halifax, near where he had grown up. Through the years he had climbed the hospital ladder, to become one of the more senior doctors in the hospital. Once the war had broken out, Canada was reluctant to force citizens to join the army. The army had already enough medics at the time, and Dr. Chase felt no urgency to leave his high-paying job, just to head overseas to help some foreigners he didn't know. Once injured soldiers had started returning to Canada, however, he had wondered if he had made the right choice. Partly because he could have proved his expertise in the field, and partly because he could have enjoyed some of the glory and glamour he thought was out there. He wasn't married and had little family, so coming home a hero would have increased his chances for more companionship. Looking back at some of the mangled and distressed soldiers that returned, he had no idea why he thought the way he did. And hearing only a few of the horrors that Henry had lived, made him again wonder why the war had seemed so exciting.

Due to the relationship that Henry had with his doctor, he was given a private room to recuperate in. Both sensed that he would only be there for a few days, but Henry was anxious to get on with finishing what he so desperately wanted to complete. Dr. Meier lay in the hospital bed, scanning the letter, feeling both excited and worried. He began to dread the final moments of his mission, but longed for it to be over. On the one hand, he had endured more hardship than he ever could have imagined, only to find the proper recipient of the young Canadian soldier's writing. On the other hand, once he had handed the letter over, it was done. He had always envisioned himself holding onto Elizabeth as she cried, and then accepting an invitation to live with her forever more. Thinking about it, it was absurd to think that was going to happen. First of all, Elizabeth might not even want the letter now. Maybe she has moved on with her life, and has married someone else. Maybe she would hate him for taking this long to deliver it, or not giving it to the English army in the first place. But, didn't she know what hardships he had faced just getting it this far? Of course not, he realized. For the absolute first time, since the whole journey began, he never thought that maybe she didn't want the letter. Elizabeth was going to be his lifelong friend, his only friend. But she was an English spinster, and he, a German ex-army doctor, who carried the emotional baggage of a lost wife and child. There was no reason for them to ever get along. Henry sighed as he thought of all the negative possibilities, after years of thinking only of the positives.

"What's the matter?" Dr. Chase asked as he walked into the room clipboard in hand. Henry looked at his doctor, not wanting to burden him with his problems, but also not wanting to share his inner thoughts, either. "Just thinking," was all that Henry said. Dr. Chase wanted to take his temperature and blood pressure as he always did, and noticed the yellowish envelope lying on the table. The inked words 'Elizabeth' still visible on the face. "Your wife?" Dr. Chase asked plainly, unaware of the situation. Henry thought for a minute, and then stopped. "No. I'm looking for her, so I can give it to her." "What's her last name?" came the obvious next question from the doctor, oblivious of the fact if Henry had known it, he probably would have contacted her by now.

"I don't know," was the only answer Henry could give, which seemed to sum up the situation clearly. Dr. Chase wrapped a plastic bandage around Henry's arms and began to pump it up, checking his blood pressure. He wasn't one to stand around without conversation, so he probed his patient further nonchalantly. "She's going to be difficult to find. Do you know where she lives?" Henry lifted the envelope up with his spare arm and held it close to him. "Here in Halifax, that's all I know." "Well, good luck with that," Dr. Chase offered, not sensing the desperation in Henry's voice. He had no idea how important it would be for him to find her. "There are probably thousands of Elizabeths in Halifax, and it's a big place."

Henry sunk to a new low. On one hand, he was happy to be free of incarceration, and healing from his numerous injuries. But he was now faced with the possibility of spending the rest of his life searching for a woman that may or may not even still be here. Was it possible that she was even alive, thought Henry suddenly? She had just lost her brother and her fiancé. Maybe she had killed herself; he could certainly understand that possibility. Had she moved? Would she stay in a house that reminded her of the losses she felt? Henry remained on the bed, while Dr. Chase finished the last of the tests. "I think you're done," the doctor told him happily. Henry's eyes flashed open, not expecting to hear that at this point in time.

"Done?" he asked his doctor.

"Done," Dr. Chase repeated. "You have a few minor abrasions that still need to be healed, but nothing that would keep you here any longer.

F leaving his small apartment above the clinic in Germany, Henry realized that he had nowhere to go. He had no house, or home to stay in. No one was waiting for him, to cook him a meal or provide him with a shower and a meal. Ever so briefly, he thought of asking his doctor if he had a place to stay, but his German stubbornness, and the lack of desire to become a constant storyteller, made him think otherwise. Dr. Chase could sense something with Henry. "What's the matter?" Henry took a deep breath, "Is there somewhere I can stay?" "You mean like a hotel or something?" the doctor asked. "Yes, something like that," Henry told him. Then quickly added, "Just until I find where to send this letter."

Dr. Chase, still oblivious to the importance of Henry's mission, gathered up the rest of his instruments and put them back in the cupboards that lined the room. "There are hotels all over, but there is a fairly inexpensive one near the edge of town, *Ocean Point Hotel* I think it's called. Funny, as it's really not that close to the ocean, but I guess it is the closest one to the ocean, on that side of town." Dr. Chase stopped suddenly realizing that he was starting to ramble. Henry lifted himself up off the bed and grabbed his small bag and coat and got ready to leave. "There is a bus stop right outside the hospital that should take you across town. Just take it all the way and then look behind you, it should be right on the corner." Dr. Chase told him without being asked. Henry was silent as he gathered up his things, not in any particular rush to head out of the hospital. For some twisted reason, he actually felt at home here. He had spent so much of his life in hospitals and clinics, either in the bed, or standing beside one. He tried to search the future, but couldn't foresee another time when he would be back to one, hopefully not as a patient, but even as a doctor.

Dr. Chase walked out of the room, something in the back of his mind nagging him. He really wondered what and where his patient was going. He should have offered a place to stay, or maybe find him a place to rent. But it seemed that if someone was so willing to endure such tragedy, and live through all that pain, he must have a plan. He really wouldn't have made the trip all the way across the ocean without one, would he? Dr. Chase pondered it for a moment, but eventually forgot about it, returning to his normal duties and his all-too-normal life.

Chapter Twenty-Three

WITH EVERY STEP he took leaving the hospital, Henry thought about what he was going to do. Elizabeth. Elizabeth. How would he find her? But wasn't he meant to find her? Wasn't that his mission? After all he had been through, God had finally released him from jail. Wasn't that the sign he needed to tell him that he would deliver her the precious letter? As he walked through the entrance of the hospital, patients, doctors, and visitors walked by, ignorant of how desperate he was feeling. He spotted the bus stop on the corner with a bus already pulled up in front of it, unsure whether he was in a hurry or not. Half-heartedly jogging toward it, he watched as the last of the passengers waiting on the corner got on, and without waiting an extra second the bus rolled forward in a puff of black smoke. Henry was left to stand all alone at the bus stop waiting for the next one to arrive.

After spending a few minutes deciphering the bus schedule, he realized that he would be waiting another hour. Another hour of thinking where he was to go, even though he wouldn't really know where to go, even if he *was* sitting in the bus right now. Over and over again, Henry wondered how he was going to find her. Could there be that many Elizabeths in a country like Nova Scotia?

After several minutes, a man walking lightly on crutches hobbled to the corner, obviously hoping to catch the same bus Henry was. Scanning the schedule wrapped around the bus stop pole, the tall skinny man turned around and walked across the street to where a telephone booth stood empty. Henry watched him, as he grabbed a book and scanned the pages until he found what he was looking for. Cursing that he didn't have the ability to zoom into what was going on, Henry squinted his eyes trying to figure out what the man on crutches was doing. "Address book," Henry exclaimed. "Of course. Elizabeth would be in there." Feeling more excited, Henry waited impatiently for the man to finish his phone call, and head back across the street to the bus stop. Henry was already waiting outside the booth, as the man on crutches replaced the phone on the receiver and exited.

Flipping through the pages of the off-white coloured phone book, Henry half expected to see her name printed on the very first page. Now Halifax wasn't a huge city, relatively speaking, especially compared to some of the metropolitan cities Henry had traveled to in Germany, but the phone book contained more names and numbers than he had anticipated. And of course, the names were listed in alphabetical order according to the last name. "Elizabeth," Henry mumbled as he flipped through the pages. "There." Henry pointed to the first Elizabeth he saw. He searched his pockets for a pen and paper, but couldn't find any. Putting his finger on the page, he figured he would keep looking to make sure that he hadn't overlooked another entry.

Now Henry was of course well educated. He had lived in good times and in bad, and had come through to see the other end. He was of course fluent in German, and spoke excellent English. He even had taken a few courses in French during his medical training. But for some reason, he was blind to the fact that it would take him days or months to track down all the names with Elizabeth in the phone book. He didn't have much more money or a place to stay. He didn't have a car or even the faintest idea where all the addresses were located in the city. All he wanted to do was find Elizabeth, and he didn't even want to think about anything else. It was when he saw the next Elizabeth, Elizabeth Marshall, and then another and then another, that he realized how stupid he was being. Then came a Lizzy, then a Liz, followed eventually by another Elizabeth. There was a Doctor Elizabeth Cummins, a Professor Elizabeth Sturdy, he even read the words, Elizabeth French's Make-up Studio. His finger still holding the place of the very first *Elizabeth* he slid it out, knowing that this would be futile.

It would seem an eternity that he had been standing in the cramp phone booth, before Henry finally succumbed to the fact that it was hopeless. All the pain and torture he had endured to find a person that he couldn't find. It was a new sense of hopelessness that he felt now. He had been on an emotional rollercoaster, just before the war had ended. He thought his life was finally coming back, when he had been released from jail. Instead of looking up to the heavens, he looked down to the ground, shuffling back to the bus stop in dejection. Could God have really saved him, just to humiliate him again with this new insurmountable obstacle? The man in crutches gave a curious glance as Henry approached him, wondering what he had been doing in the bus stop for so long. Henry stopped in front him, in desperation.

"Do you know Elizabeth?" Henry asked him, for no other reason, than he was at the end of his rope. "Elizabeth?" the man asked curiously, hearing the accent in Henry's voice. Henry hadn't the heart to probe further. "Sorry, sir I don't know any Elizabeth," the man finally said, turning to stand in the opposite corner of the bus stop.

What Henry didn't know was that this man had served briefly in the army, overseas in France, before severely injuring his knee. It had been a long, hard recovery process that still plagued him to this day, all due to a German soldier that had lodged more than a few bullets into his leg and knee. Whatever or whomever this German was looking for, was no concern of his, and even if he knew this *Elizabeth*, she was better off not knowing this one. Henry slunk down on the bench, letting his failures fall on him heavily; he barely noticed the bus as it screeched to a halt in front of him. He threw in what coins he had, not caring if it was the exact amount or not, and sat down in the back with his head leaned against the dirty window facing the curb.

As the bus drove through the streets of Halifax, making stop after stop, Henry tried hard to block out the frustration and fear that welled up inside. People and cars whirred by. More and more people who could be Elizabeth flew by the window, making Henry's emotions go as low as they could go. There was no way that he would find her. There was no way he could find her. The bus driver yelled, "Last stop!" and pulled over.

Without thinking Henry exited and turned to face the opposite street. As the bus pulled away, the promised building, 'Ocean Point Hotel' revealed itself. Henry hadn't the desire to go anywhere. He merely sat on the bench, and clutched the letter he removed from his cloak. With little else to do, he removed the very familiar letter within the envelope, and scanned it again. He hadn't read it that many times, but the words clung to his memory like glue. He could almost recite the entire letter, verbatim. Looking at the familiar handwriting in front of him, he turned the page to read the last words on the page.

Before I go, let me tell you one last thing. I love you. I will find you. I promise that I will find you. This letter is all that I have left to tell you that, and I know that it will find you too. It has to. It just has to.

Your Love

Henry could only sigh and wish that his life would end. He had tried it once and failed, but maybe now he would do it again for real. He had taken someone's promise and smashed it to pieces. He had caused so much pain and loneliness. He had done that all by himself.

Caressing the creases in the letter, he found no other solution. He had failed.

"God," Henry mouthed almost silently. "I've failed."

Henry looked up to where he had seen the hotel, wondering if it would be there, that he would end it all. But what he noticed instead was another building standing beside it. He had seen a building like this before. He saw it and stood before it, thinking only of his desire not to enter. He had maliciously left it, to do what he thought was best. Maybe in some sort of defiant way he could end it all there. There would be some sort of crooked justice in it, Henry thought. Jingling the remaining marks in his pants pocket and the odd Canadian coin he had left, Henry chose a direction.

Skirting through the light traffic to face the front of the building, Henry walked through the open door and under the sign that read, *St. Joseph*. Walking softly and gently, he put down his bag of clothes in the foyer, and was drawn to the large cross that hung in the front. Walking right to the front he stared at its wooden corners, and wondered what would happen next. "This was it," he thought and prayed. "Now what?" Standing for several minutes he knew that no answer would come. He knew that God had steered him clear of any answers he so desperately needed. God had given him a reprieve in the jail cell, only to mock him now that he had nowhere to go. The lone German doctor stood at the front of the church, wanting to run out and scream, find a place to crawl under and die. But all he could do was stand there and stare at the old and cracked stained cross that hung in front of him. "I've left my home, my country, my wife, my child and my life to come here. I've done everything I thought I should," Henry mumbled under his breath, feeling his cheeks get warm and redden with anger. "You want to help me, then you don't do anything. What do you want? Why can't you just leave me alone to die?"

The lady sitting in the seat next to him looked over at him, wondering who was calling to the wooden cross as desperately as she was. Henry remembered the rubble lying on top of his beautiful wife and child, he remembered the young soldier lying on his table, breathing his last breath. He felt the blows that hit him in the jail cell. And now he felt his heart ache with a sadness that he never wanted to feel, and wanted it to stop. With little life left inside him, and no more energy to continue, he turned to sit. "Excuse me," he said to the lady who sat there. She didn't say anything but glanced ever so briefly at him, then tucked in her legs to let him sit beside her.

Henry sat down heavily, still clutching the letter now tucked back inside the envelope. He held it in front of him, turning it over and over each time very silently reading the word, 'Elizabeth' as it became visible. He looked over to see the woman beside him, and noticed that she seemed as desperate as he. He noticed a tear drift slowly from her eye, only to feel one of the same, fall from his. Looking in her direction, he saw her rub her hands over and over, caressing scars that seemed so out of place on her wrists. Henry couldn't help but raise his left arm to his neck to caress the scars he had inflicted on himself. She looked over at him briefly, not wanting to be noticed, and spied the envelope now flipping over in the strange man's hands. She had barely the courage to say anything, feeling a lump in her throat she tried to swallow down, but curiosity overwhelmed her. Without looking directly at the man beside her, she asked a simple inquiring question that would change their two lives forever, summarized in one word.

"Elizabeth?"

Postscript

As the two of them crested a small hill, large oak trees stretching their branches out into the street as if escorting them on their way, Lizzy's arm intertwined with Henry's. She leaned on him as they walked, looking like a pair of friends that had known each other forever and a day. As they passed over a small summit in the road, the old house emerged into view in the distance, surrounded by the sound and smell of ocean waves crashing far behind it. The familiar salty breeze blew on their faces, and Henry was beginning to love the feel of it. He took a deep breath and let the air cling to him, as he thought what a wonderful sensation it was. Small droplets of water clung to his cheeks, and while the physical feeling was similar to the many tears he had shed for so many years, it was a much more beautiful feeling now on his cheeks and in his heart.

The house though, looked aged and worn; more than Henry had realized. Dark moldy shingles hung loosely from the roof, and paint from the badly worn fence was peeling badly. Weeds poked out from the ground at every turn, strangling what was left of the lawn and garden, rising up from the dirt to choke out life from everything that tried to grow beside it. "I'm afraid it needs a lot of work," Elizabeth said sadly. "I'm sorry I didn't take better care of it." They walked slowly, not feeling in any rush to get to their destination, just enjoying the journey together.

"I'm afraid I'm not much of a handyman." Henry smiled, letting Lizzy tighten her grip on his arm. Lizzy stopped suddenly, and turned to the side to cough. She quickly wrenched her arm free of Henry and brought her handkerchief up to her mouth as she coughed violently again. Catching her breath, she looked into her white handkerchief and spotted a tiny fleck of blood lying in the middle of it. Henry saw it too.

Finally calmed down, she returned her arm to his, and started to walk again. "I can take care of *you* though," Henry stated, gingerly removing a few strands of hair from her face with his other hand. Lizzy smiled without looking at him, knowing that she would never feel alone again. Henry could never replace her fiancé or her brother, or even her departed pastor, but he felt just as close to her somehow. Maybe their two separate and life changing journeys, that brought them together, had formed a friendship beyond their comprehension.

"We reap what we sow, "Elizabeth said finally, feeling the handkerchief in her pocket. "I'm hoping we do." Henry replied, pressing her close to him, again feeling the tears that had been welled up inside him let go. He didn't mind. After so long a time it was refreshing to show his emotions being reflected by the salty drops trickling down his cheeks, both salt from the ocean and salt from his eyes mixing together in harmony.

As they washed down his face, he remembered Carmen and Eden. He didn't feel sad or angry, only relief. He could finally let them go. He still loved them so much, and would think of them daily, but he could concentrate now on another relationship. An important relationship. He looked down to Lizzy's hand, which rested close beside him, and saw the clenched fist that held the letter he had carried for so long. He smiled with satisfaction. While the letter would stay at her side for many days and be read over and over, it wasn't the contents of the letter that was so important now, but where it had led him. Without it, he would have never undertaken such a journey, and never found the person to fill the hole in his heart. Henry looked up to the heavens with a renewed acknowledgment, and mouthed the words, "Thank you." He had already filled the hole in his soul.

Looking back to Lizzy, and catching her smiling secretly, he repeated,

"I'm hoping we do."

Lizzy rested her head on his shoulder, as the two of them, from such different lives and from opposite sides of the world, walked towards the rest of their lives.

www.ingramcontent.com/pod-product-compliance
Lightning Source LLC
LaVergne TN
LVHW011827060526
838200LV00053B/3930